I0684689

10 SEXY STORIES IN 1

Naughty Wives

JUST PLAIN BOB

EROTICA SHORT STORIES, VOL. 29

WARNING

This book contains sexually explicit scenes and adult language. It may be considered offensive to some readers. This book is for sale to adults ONLY.

Please store your files wisely where they cannot be accessed by underage readers.

About the Publisher

4Fun Publishing, a member of **BLVNP Incorporated**, 340 S. Lemon #6200, Walnut CA 91789, info@blvnp.com / legal@blvnp.com
NOTE: Due to the highly emotional reaction of some people to works of erotic fiction, any email sent to the above address that contains foul language or religious references is automatically deleted by our anti-spam software and will not be seen. All other communications are welcome.

DISCLAIMER

Please don't be stupid and kill yourself. This book is a work of FICTION. Do not try any new sexual practice that you find in this book. It is fiction and not to be confused with reality. Neither the author nor the publisher or its associates assume any responsibility for any loss, injury, death or legal consequences resulting from acting on the contents in this book. Every character in this book is over 18 years of age. The author's opinions are not to be construed as the opinions of the publisher. The material in this book is for entertainment purposes ONLY. Enjoy.

Erotica Short Stories, Vol.29
Naughty Wives
9 Sexy Stories in 1

By: Just Plain Bob

© **Just Plain Bob 2015**
ISBN: 978-1-68030-406-0

Rob And Aggie

Momma's Boys

Stephanie Anne

Merrily The Maid

New Slut In Town

Martha's Revenge

Sticking It To Peggy

The Ex Wants a Favor

The Wedding, The Funeral

Rob And Aggie

I met Agnes in the ninth grade, started dating her and we were pretty much an established couple from the tenth grade on. We had no problems all the way through high school and – cliché of all clichés – we exchanged our virginities the night of the senior prom. Once we discovered sex, we were at it every chance we got.

We had been talking about getting married since the eleventh grade and we had decided that we would wait until we finished college before tying the knot.

College changed Aggie. In high school our peers recognized that we were a couple and the guys left Aggie alone, but those same circumstances didn't hold once we got to college. While there were some old classmates from our high school there, the majority of students were from other places and the guys didn't see Aggie as my girl. They saw her as a desirable female and she was constantly being hit on.

I knew it was happening, but there wasn't much I could do about it. We had different majors and took different classes so we usually only saw each other in the evenings after classes and after I got off work. The attention had an effect on Aggie. She became more 'flirty' for lack of a better word. Several times I saw her walking with other guys, smiling and talking with them, but I was on the other side of the quad and she didn't notice me.

Twice I took a shortcut through the Student Union on my way from one class to another and I saw Aggie in the cafeteria; once with a guy and once with two of them. It never registered on me until much, much later that I never saw her with other girls. It was always with guys.

It never worried me. We were a couple right? We were in love right? We were planning on getting married right? So nothing for me to sweat right? She was a great looking girl so naturally she attracted guys, but she was mine and she proved it every night when we got together.

***

Four years later we graduated, found jobs in our fields of study, got married and began a life of wedded bliss. I was the poster boy for 'fat, dumb and happy' for almost six years before the balloon popped. It was an accident that brought about my rude awakening.

I was sitting at my desk at work when Molly from the mailroom put some files in my in basket. I picked up the top one and started going through it. I wondered why it had been routed to me since it concerned an account that Wally Bergman was handling. Wally was an old classmate from high school and college. I was halfway through it when I spotted a major error. A quick calculation in my head told me that the projections were off almost three million dollars. I was reaching for my calculator to work out the exact figure when Wally came rushing into my office and asked me if I had seen the file.

"I've got to make copies of it and be ready to give the Apex people a presentation in half an hour."

"I have the file right here. I don't know why I have it; I guessed that someone wanted me to look it over so I did, but I don't think that you want to present this to Apex."

I showed him what I'd found and even though I know it is usually only a figure of speech I'd swear to it that his face went white.

"Jesus Rob, this could have cost me my job. I need to do a quick re-work on it" and he took the file and hurried off.

It was a Thursday and Aggie always had to work late on Thursdays to get payroll out for the Friday payday so I did my usual and hit Bud's Bar after work for his half pound ground round and a couple of beers before heading home.

I'd just finished my burger and was starting on my second beer when Wally came in, saw me and joined me in my booth. He ordered a beer from Sue and told her to give him my bill.

"It's the least I can do after you saved my ass today."

I didn't argue with him over it since we weren't talking big money and we sat and talked about work for a bit and then some "Have you seen (fill in the blank) and a little of "Have you heard what (fill in the blank) did" and then Wally turned my world upside down and inside out.

"I have to ask you this Rob. It is none of my business and I know it, but you are a nice guy and I really like you. I'd like to know why you put up with Aggie's shit."

"I don't know what you mean Wally."

"Why do you let her fuck around on you?"

"What the hell are you talking about Wally?"

He took one look at my face and his paled and he said, "Oh fuck! You didn't know."

He started to get up, but I grabbed him and pulled him back down.

"No you don't Wally. You don't drop a bomb like that on me and then get up and run. Sit back down and spill it."

He sat down and said, "I don't know what to say Rob."

"Just tell it Wally. Just spit it out."

"I thought you knew Rob. I mean it has been what, ten years, and you don't know? My God Rob; how could you not know?"

"Know what Wally?"

"That Aggie is a round heeled slut."

I just stared at him, unable to ask a single question.

"I'm sorry Rob; I wish I'd never opened my mouth."

I shook off my mental paralysis and said, "But you did Wally so now you have to finish it. How do you know and how long have you known?"

"I've known since our senior year in high school and I know because I'm one of the many who did her."

I was stunned at the information, but I had a crying need to know.

"Start at the beginning Wally and don't leave anything out. Please don't leave anything out."

The story that unfolded was shocking to me. Not only the content, but the fact that it had been going on for over ten years and I hadn't had a clue. Not even a wisp of one.

Two weeks after the senior prom Wally had gone over to his cousin's house and as was his habit he just walked into the house and headed for George's bedroom where he knew George would be on his computer. But George wasn't on the computer. He was on and in Aggie. Wally stood there watching them and they both saw him and since neither one of them yelled at him to get out, he undressed and waited his turn.

He and George took turns fucking Aggie until she called a halt to the proceedings. She said she had to get cleaned up and meet me when I got off work from my part time job at Jessup's Market. He and George fucked her off and on whenever I was at work until George met and got serious with Melody Martin. She fucked Wally for a couple of weeks and then one day when he stopped to see her she was already fucking Mike Bellah and Justin Walsh and he undressed and joined in. All three of them worked on her until she had to stop so she could meet me. Wally shared her with several other guys and many times she had pulled trains with more than a half dozen guys present.

"I know that we were friends and all, but it wasn't like we were best friends you know? And you remember how it was when we were eighteen and had pussy on the brain. You guys were kind of going steady, but I didn't think the two of you were all that serious anyway. I mean if you were really serious would she be fucking anybody who showed her a hard cock? And it didn't change when we started college."

"As I remember it freshman first semester she had classes Monday/Thursday and Tuesday/Friday and didn't have any classes on Wednesday. Her last class on Monday/Thursday let out at two and her last class on Tuesday/Friday let out at one. I don't remember your schedule, but when you got out of class you went to work and when Aggie got out of class she was off to a bedroom somewhere. Wednesday was like an all-day fuck-a-thon.

"It was like that all the way through school Rob. Class schedules changed from term to term, but the constant was Aggie spreading after class and until you got off work. I'm making it sound like it was every day, but it wasn't. Two or three times a week though. Most of us guys were shocked when you and Aggie married. We just knew that you had to know what she had been doing, but you married her anyway. A lot of us thought that maybe you were one of those guys who got off on your women doing other men. Tyler thought that maybe you and Aggie were swingers, but no one ever remembered seeing you with another girl, but we were always seeing Aggie with other guys."

"I had no fucking idea Wally. Not even the whisper of an idea."

"Damn Rob; I'm sorry to be the one to clue you in, but since you never knew it stands to reason that you probably don't know that she has a standing Thursday night date with Bob and Bill Howard. The Tuesday you bowl she sees Mark Willard. I don't know who else she sees and when, but it is a sure bet that anytime you are off somewhere doing something so is Aggie. Not that it matters much, but I did stop doing her when you got married. Single pussy is one thing, but messing around with married pussy is something totally different."

"I don't know what to say Wally. And I don't know what I'm going to do, but I'm sure as hell going to do something."

I polished off my beer and stood up to leave. I stopped and turned to Wally.

"Thanks Wally. Thanks for the burger, the beer and for pulling my head out of my ass."

***

As I drove home I was rolling what Wally had told me around in my head. Did I believe what he told me? On the one hand I said "No way! Aggie loves me and she wouldn't do that to me." On the other hand was the question "Why would Wally lie to me?" I had to finally admit to myself that he wouldn't. He knew I'd check out what he'd told me and if he had lied how would we be able to keep working together? The answer was that we wouldn't be able to and Wally knew it. It was going to be hard enough to work with him knowing about him and Aggie, but we would eventually get by it because I did remember what it was like to be a teen and have pussy on the brain and I knew that if some other guy's girl had offered me her pussy back then and I didn't have Aggie, I'd have taken it.

The real question was "What the fuck do you do now Rob?" I did know that Aggie and I were through. I could maybe – just maybe – have gotten by a one night drunken mistake or maybe even a short term affair if Aggie could convince me that it would never happen again, but outright slutdom for ten years? No fucking way!!!

I was in bed pretending to be asleep when Aggie got home from 'getting out the payroll' and I ignored her when her hand touched my cock. The bitch wanted to give me sloppy seconds and I wasn't going for it. Admittedly I'd been getting them for years and it hadn't killed me, but I didn't know it at the time. I did now though and the touch of her hand on my cock made my skin crawl and for the first time ever, I didn't get an erection when Aggie handled me.

I was up before Aggie in the morning and I had the coffee on and was reading the morning paper when Aggie came down.

"What happened to you last night? I came home horny and eager and you were already in bed. That isn't like you Rob."

"Something that I ate didn't agree with me and I was feeling poorly and so I went to bed early."

"Well I certainly hope that you are better today. I'm going to need you to do double duty tonight to make up for last night."

As soon as I got to work I called Felix Mather. Felix was a friend from high school and was now an attorney practicing corporate law (whatever that was) and I asked him to recommend a 'take no prisoners' divorce lawyer.

"Shit!" he said.

"What does that mean?"

"It means that what I'd hoped was true isn't. That you are looking for a divorce lawyer means that what I thought you and Aggie had is not what you and Aggie have and that you have finally found out about her."

"What did you think we had?"

"An open marriage of some type. How else could Aggie do what she was doing and still be with you? I mean it was obvious to everyone that you were devoted to her and how could that be unless you were okay with what she was doing?"

"Believe it or not Felix I had no clue as to what she was doing until yesterday."

Felix was silent for a couple of seconds and then said, "Give Tom Sweet a call and tell him I sent you." I called Sweet and told him that Felix recommended him and he told me that he could see me that day if I could be there at one. I told him I could make it and I did.

Sweet told me that my options ranged from an amicable split to an Attila the Hun scorched earth policy. We were not a no fault state and adultery was an acceptable grounds for divorce.

"But to go for a divorce using adultery as grounds you need to have irrefutable evidence. Hearsay won't do it."

"How do I get the evidence that I need?"

He took a card out of his desk and handed it to me. It read "Gaston Marshell, Private investigator."

"His office is just across the street. If you want I can give him a call and see if he can get you in right away."

"Please do. I want to get this over with as soon as possible. Go ahead and start the divorce paperwork and I'll get the evidence to you as soon as I get it."

Sweet made the call and ten minutes later Gaston Marshall was telling me what we needed to do. Unfortunately one of the things I needed to do was act completely natural around Aggie and not give her any reason to suspect that I wasn't still the clueless clown she was accustomed to.

"And as distasteful as it may be to you," Marshall said, "It means no changes in your routine. If you have sex three or four times a week you have to do it. If you are usually the instigator you will need to do it. Just remember that you are no longer making love; you are just getting your rocks off. Do not do anything that might make her change her routine in any way. It is important to us and what we want to happen that she be clueless of the fact that there has been a change in your relationship."

I went back to my office and bit the bullet and called Aggie at work. It was our habit to go out for dinner every Friday night and for breakfast every Sunday morning so when I got her to the phone I asked her if Tricocci's was okay for dinner and she said it was.

While I was eating my Veal Marcella and Aggie was working on her Rigatoni and sipping white wine employees of Marshall Investigations were placing wireless cameras and listening devices in the house. As I took a sip of my Merlot I was running over Marshall's words to me.

"It is natural that you will try to spot the hidden cameras, but you have to fight the urge. If she notices you doing it there is a chance that all of our efforts will be wasted. The other thing you will need to do is force yourself to act natural in the bedroom and that is not going to be an easy thing for you to do unless you are a born exhibitionist. The system is sound and motion activated and you will be on camera knowing that it is likely that some of my employees will see you. You cannot let that inhibit you.

"There is a switch that will allow you to turn off the system when you are at home, but experience has shown that most will forget to turn the switch back on when they leave the house. My advice to you is leave the system alone and try and pretend that you are a porn star at work making a porn tape."

After dinner I asked Aggie if she wanted to go for a few drinks and maybe some dancing and she told me no.

"We need to get home so you can make it up to me for letting me down last night."

On the way home she slid over next to me, unzipped me and took out my cock.

"Drive carefully sweetie. Don't hit anything that might make me bite off your dick."

When she took me in her mouth it was a good thing that her head was buried in my lap so she couldn't see the grimace on my face when her lips surrounded my cock. In my mind what she was doing was not something special for me, but what she had done with a hundred other cocks over the last ten years. But disgusted as I might be with Aggie human nature took over a couple of minutes into things and my cock throbbed and wanted her to continue on and get me off. I punched a load into her mouth just as I turned into our driveway and Aggie swallowed it, licked me clean and then told me to hurry up and get up to the bedroom.

I couldn't follow Marshall's advice. No way could I act natural knowing that I might be fucking for an audience. It was going to be a chore just trying to act natural as I fucked Aggie so I went to where I was told the switch would be and I shut the system off. I left my cell phone on the seat of the car knowing that when I saw it when I went to leave the house it would remind me to turn the system back on.

I don't know if it registered on Aggie or not, but I didn't make love to her that night; I fucked her. Unfortunately once was not enough and I had to perform two more times before Aggie would let me go to sleep.

I got up in the morning and dressed to go for my morning run and before I left Aggie reminded me that she wouldn't be there when I got back.

"I'll be having my hair done, but I should be home by two."

I had always wondered why her hair appointment took from nine in the morning until two in the afternoon. Aggie said that it was because she got to gossiping with the other regulars and usually ended up going to lunch with them. It could even be the truth, but after what I'd recently found out I was thinking that she probably met one of her fuck buddies either before or after getting her hair done.

On my way out I turned the switch for the system back on. I doubted that anything would happen while I was on my run, but I needed to get into the habit of making sure that the system was on when I wasn't home. The switch only shut off the cameras. The listening devices and the phone tap were always on.

I did my usual five miles and when I got back to the house I went down into the basement and opened up the cabinet above my work bench. It is where I told Marshall to put the recorders. I figured that it was the best location since Aggie rarely went into the basement and almost never went into my work area. There were two receivers in the cabinet. One was for the listening devices and phone tap and the other was a DVD recorder that received the input from the wireless cameras. I checked the recorder for the phone tap and had my suspicions confirmed.

"Hello?"

"Good morning lover. Are we still on for today?"

"You bet. The wife took the kids to the zoo so we have until six tonight."

"You know I can't stay that long. I need to be home by two. Any later and it might get Rob to wondering. He has already questioned that fact that I don't get home until two."

"Then skip the hair job and get over here so we can make it

happen."

"Yeah. Sure. Then what do I tell Rob when he asks why I've been gone so long and my hair hasn't been done. I want more time with you too baby, but we have to settle for what we can get."

I recognized the man's voice. It was my cousin Lou. I was steaming when I went back upstairs and wondering how many of my other relatives she had fucked or was fucking. I was able to get my anger under control by the time Aggie got home from her 'hair appointment' and was able to hold it together. An hour after she got home I faked a fall down the basement stairs and told Aggie that I'd hurt my back.

"Must have pulled a muscle or something."

That took care of having to fuck her for the next couple of days at least.

***

Monday I called Aggie at work and told her that I was going to be going out of town on Tuesday and would be gone until Friday and that I'd be home in time to take her out to dinner. There was no trip of course. It might be a wasted three days, but I didn't think so. I travelled on the average of once a month and Aggie was always home when I made my nightly check in phone call. Since my calls were at irregular times – anywhere from seven to ten – I doubted that she waited for my calls and then went out so if she was fucking around on me as much as I had been led to believe she was probably doing it on our bed as I was talking to her. That was my hope anyway. If she was and the cameras caught it I would have what my attorney wanted in the way of 'irrefutable proof' for the divorce action.

That evening Aggie wanted to make love.

"I need something to hold me for the three nights you will be gone."

Yeah! Right! Fortunately for me at least my back was still hurting so I had to beg off. Tuesday morning Aggie kissed me goodbye and suitcase in hand, I left the house for my business trip. I drove to work and got in almost a full day. I left at three and drove to our neighborhood and parked a block over from the house. Using my laptop I punched in a code that Marshall had given me that activated the software he had loaded onto my computer. A few keystrokes and I was listening to the recorder on the phone line.

"Hello?"

"Hey sexy hunk; it's me."

"What's up?"

"Hubby just left on a three day trip. You ready to spend three fun filled nights with me?"

"Does a duck walk barefoot on the beach?"

"I'll take that as a yes. I leave it to you to call Tony. I've got to get out of here and get to work. I'll be home by six."

"See you then."

I shut down the computer and called Tom Sweet and told him to have the papers ready to serve by Thursday and then I told him how I wanted it done. He told me that to do it that way would cost me more than the standard service fee and I told him that I didn't care. I left the neighborhood and drove to the other side of town and checked into a motel. It had a restaurant and a bar just next door and I settled in for a three day stay.

I liked the bar. It was my kind of place and every time I went there it put a big smile on my face (apologies to Toby Keith). It was a country/western bar and the juke box was loaded with good tunes to dance to and every night I stopped there I saw three or four unattached ladies who couldn't stand to see a man sitting alone while there was music to dance to being played.

The first time I was there I was sitting at the bar nursing a long neck where a great looking redhead came up to me and said:

"Come on sugar; they're playing our song" and she took my hand, pulled me off the bar stool and led me out onto the dance floor. As I took her in my arms and started the waltz she said:

"Don't get the wrong idea sugar. I'm not tolling. I just love to dance and you were there."

Her name was Rhonda and after the dance she invited me to join her and her two friends, Laura and Shelby, at their table. I spent until ten-thirty taking turns dancing with them and then I told them I had to call it a night.

"Maybe we will see you again," Rhonda said. "We are in here two or three nights a week."

"I'm just next door in the motel so it is likely that I will be in here the next two nights."

I went to bed in a good mood for the first time since my talk with Wally.

***

The next afternoon at three I was parked a block over from the house and watching what the wireless cameras had picked up the night before. The two guys who joined Aggie in the bedroom were young guys. They were at least six years younger than Aggie and I wondered if it was youthful exuberance that Aggie was after. The content was nothing exceptional. It was just plain sucking and fucking although it was a bit strange seeing my wife double teamed.

The visuals of Aggie fucking the two guys didn't really interest me. What I wanted was the audio. I was surprised at what I heard or more to the point what I didn't hear. I expected to hear Aggie ridiculing me and my lovemaking skills or lack thereof, but she never did shoot me through the grease. It was the same Wednesday. The only time I was mentioned was when one of the guys said that he wished they could get together more often. Aggie told him that she was sorry, but that I had first call on her time.

What I did pick up was Aggie telling them that they had to be out of the house by six in the morning.

"None of the neighbors are early risers so I need you to be gone before they get up and see you leaving."

Both Wednesday and Thursday morning they left the house right at six and I assumed that it would be the same on Friday. I called my attorney and had him change the serving of the papers until Friday.

At five forty-five Friday morning I was parked just down the street from the house. At five fifty-five the front door opened and the two guys came out. They turned to say goodbye to Aggie who was standing just inside the door and that is when they saw the man standing just off to the side. He stepped in front of the open door, served Aggie and then turned and walked away leaving Aggie and her two fuck buddies looking at his back. I pulled up in front of the house and honked the horn to make sure that I had Aggie's attention and then I waved "Bye bye" and drove off."

***

In the papers that were served on Aggie was a letter from me to her. Basically it said that I never wanted to speak to her again unless it was in the presence of our attorneys. I didn't want to know why. I didn't want to hear that she loved only me and it was just meaningless sex with the others. I didn't want to hear that it wasn't what I thought it was and I didn't want to hear that we could get by it because of our love for each other. I did not want to hear any of the garbage that cheaters come up with to try and excuse their actions when they get caught.

Of course Aggie paid no attention to the letter and fifteen minutes after I had pulled away from the house my cell rang and it was Aggie. I let it go to voice mail along with the next seven calls from her. When I got to work I told my secretary that I had left Aggie and not to put any calls from her through. I had another thought as I was opening my office door and I turned back to her.

"Another thing Martha. If she shows up here please tell her that I'm not here. Tell her I've gone to meet with a customer."

Martha stuck her head in the door five minutes later.

"I talked to Iris on the front desk. If your wife shows up she will call me and stall your wife to give you time to get out the side door. You can go to the café and have coffee until she leaves."

I thanked her and as she went back to her desk I thought, and not for the first time, that a good secretary is a priceless thing to have.

Aggie called my cell seventeen times that day and I didn't take any of the calls. At lunch time I called my dad and brother and let them know what was going on. I told dad to tell mom and ask her to refrain from trying to get me to sit down and work things out with Aggie and he told me that he would see what he could do. It would be hard because my mom looked on Aggie as the daughter she never had.

At the end of the day I still had some work that needed to be done and since I didn't have to hurry home I decided to stay and finish it up. At five Martha told me that she was leaving and would see me in the morning.

"And by the way; your wife called five times before noon and each time I told her that I had instructions not to put her through to you.

I think she finally got the message since she hasn't called since."

I finished around seven and when I got to the lobby of course Iris was gone and Hank, our night watchman, was sitting at the reception desk and saw me and said:

"Hot time on the town tonight with the Mrs.?"

"Why would you think that?"

"She is out there waiting on you."

"We are getting a divorce Hank and she wants to talk and I don't. If she knocks on the door don't open it and if she uses the intercom tell her that you are alone in the building and that when you came to work there was a note in the turnover log that my car was in the lot because I couldn't get it started and that the towing company would be here in the morning to take it to the shop. Can do?"

"No problem Mr. Byrns. Sorry to hear it. Divorces ain't no fun. Know that cause I've had two of them."

"I'm going out the back door and avoid her."

I went out the back door, went around the block, crossed the street and walked down the alley to the back door of Dave's Diner and went in and took a seat. I sat where I could see Aggie waiting by my car. I ordered the special and kept an eye on her while I ate. I was halfway through my dessert when she went up to the building and pressed the call button on the intercom. Hank apparently told her what I'd asked him to because she went back to her car and left. I finished dessert, had one more cup of coffee and then left. I stopped in the bar for a beer or two and even thought there were a couple of ladies there alone hoping for a dance partner I had my two beers and left.

***

Saturday morning was a busy one for me as I ran around and did all the things I should have done before serving Aggie. I just hoped that I wasn't too late and she hadn't gotten around to doing what I should have done. I hit the bank and cleaned out all the accounts and took the certificates of deposit and my personal papers out of the safe deposit box, but left all of Aggie's stuff in it. I took off my wedding ring and dropped it in the box for her to find.

I hit the Waffle House for breakfast and while there I used my cell phone to call and take care of the credit cards. There were only two that were joint and I cancelled them both. That left me with a Visa and an American Express that were in my name only. Aggie also had two in her name only so all I really accomplished was make sure she couldn't run up the joint cards by taking out cash advances.

When I finished breakfast, I drove back to the motel, parked my car and called a cab to take me to the nearest Avis rental place. I rented the cheapest car they had and went back to the motel. I spent the afternoon lounging by the motel pool and reading a book.

Just before I went to eat I turned on my cell phone and checked for messages. There were nine and all from Aggie. I cleared them and then turned the phone back off. I had a light dinner and then headed for the bar.

The bar had a live band on Friday and Saturday and the place was packed. I found a seat at the bar and ordered a beer. I'd downed about half of it when I felt a tug on my shirt. I turned and saw Rhonda standing there.

"Hey cowboy. Why are you sitting here when there is a seat at our table for you?"

"Didn't see you what with the crowd and all. To be honest about it had I seen you I wouldn't have intruded on you. It would have seemed like I was taking things for granted."

"Nonsense. Come on."

I got up and followed her to her table and saw that Laura and Shelby were also there. I sat down, said hi to the girls and then said:

"There seems to be something wrong with this picture. Three stone foxes sitting at a table alone and you aren't swamped with guys? You had to come and get me? That just ain't right."

"We get a lot of attention, but it is usually from assholes. They see us here, notice the wedding rings and think that we are here looking for some guy for the night. Just three sluts out looking to cheat on their husbands. We are just here because we want to dance and only a couple of guys understand that and accept it. The rest think they are God's gift to women and we have to fight them off. After the other night we know that you are one of the good guys and you have an open invitation to join us whenever you come in and we are here."

"It isn't any of my business and I know it so feel free to tell me that, but I have to ask. Why are three gorgeous married women spending time in a place like this without your husbands?"

"It is a legitimate question," Rhonda said. "Laura's husband is in the Army Reserve and his unit was sent to Afghanistan. She was going nuts cooped up in her house alone so we decided to get her out. Shelby's husband works afternoons and my hubby is a long haul trucker and is gone a lot so the three of us banded together to keep each other company. We love to dance and here we are. What's your story? I noticed that you had a ring on last time we saw you and now it is gone."

"I served my wife with divorce papers yesterday morning and took the ring off and left it where she would find it."

"Do you feel that frees you up to hunt?"

"Not in the least. The grounds were adultery and I have no intention of doing anything that she can use for grounds in a counter suit."

"Goodie," Lara said. "We have a safe dancing partner."

I spent the rest of the evening until closing time taking turns dancing with the three of them and sharing them with the occasional guy they said yes to.

***

Sunday I spent a quiet day beside the pool with a book and Monday I drove the rental car to work. My hope was that Aggie wouldn't see my car and would think I was out of town again and stay away.

The week went by with me getting anywhere from six to ten calls a day from Aggie which I never took. Twice she called me from numbers I didn't recognize and when I answered and heard her voice I hung up on her. I stopped by the bar every night after dinner and had a beer or two. Rhonda, Laura and Shelby were there on Wednesday and Friday and I joined them. I danced with them until ten on Wednesday and until closing on Friday.

I figured that by Saturday Aggie would have figured out that I wasn't going to talk to her so I turned in my rental and drove my car to work on Monday. Bad move on my part. Monday she was parked next to my car when I came out of the building. When she saw me coming she got out of her car and was standing by my car's driver's side door. She said, "We need to talk Rob" when I got to the car. I ignored her and she moved to block the door.

"Come on Rob; you need to let me explain."

I pushed her out of the way and she stumbled and almost fell and by the time she had regained her balance I was in the car. I rolled the window down and said:

"You need to go back and read the letter that was with the divorce papers Aggie. I will not talk to you unless my attorney is present and even then all I will talk about is the details of the divorce."

"I don't want a divorce Rob."

"And I don't want you Aggie. We are done. Accept it because I'm not going to change my mind."

I rolled the window up and drove off leaving her standing there. That Aggie wasn't going to accept my refusal to talk to her became apparent to me when I got off work Tuesday.

When I walked up to my car two guys came up to me and each took hold of one of my arms. I recognized them as the two that had fucked Aggie in our bedroom. One of them said:

"Don't do anything stupid old man and you won't get hurt. Miss Aggie says she wants to talk to you and you are being obstinate so we are taking you to her. The easy way or the hard way, but you are coming with us."

Old man? I was only six or maybe seven years older than they were. They must have thought that since I was wearing a suit and a tie and carrying a briefcase I was some soft old guy. I figured that I could take them. They wouldn't be expecting the 'old guy' to do anything against the two of them so surprise should let me get one of them out of the way and one on one I was pretty sure that I could take the other one. Either way the fracas would draw attention and their little kidnapping caper would be in the shit can.

But then I thought do I really want to? If Aggie was going to go to those lengths just to get to talk to me what would she try next if I sent these two back to her all bloodied up? I allowed them to push me into my car and I sat between them, briefcase on my lap, as I was driven to the house. They escorted me inside and Aggie told them to sit me down in a chair and make sure that I stayed there. She turned to me and said:

"We are not getting a divorce!"

When she said that I started to get up from the chair, but the two guys pushed me back down and held me there as one of them said:

"You will stay put if you know what is good for you."

"We are going to stay married," Aggie said, "But there will be a few changes in the way we live. I'm sorry that you found out about my medical problem, but now that you know you are going to have to live with it. I love you. Believe it or not I love you and I'm not letting you go."

"Medical problem? What medical problem?"

"I have nymphomania. I have been a nymphomaniac since high school. You unleashed it when you took my virginity."

"Nonsense. They have drugs that can treat that sort of thing."

"Yes they do and I've tried them all. They make me sluggish and stupid and I don't like sitting around looking like a retard. Besides, I like being a nympho. I love to fuck and you should know that. Lord knows I hardly ever leave you alone. And what I do doesn't hurt you in the least. I love you and I spoil you rotten. So what if I let someone have what you couldn't use anyway. If you could stay hard 24/7 I wouldn't need anyone else, but you can't and I need it so I give the excess to others. I don't love them; I love you and I always come home to you.

"Here is the way it is going to be. I have written up a post nuptial agreement where you agree to my having as many lovers as I require to keep my sanity. You agree to leave the marriage with nothing if you later decide you don't want to continue the marriage under those conditions."

"And in exchange what do I get besides a whore for a wife?"

"You get the same loving wife you have had for the past six years and you know full well that you considered those years perfect. You considered our marriage and our life perfect even though the entire time I was doing what you now have a problem with. All that is wrong now is that your ego is involved. Someone else is using something that you have always considered yours and yours alone. You just need to accept that our life will continue the same as it has for the last six years. You need to accept that it does not mean that you are not man enough for me. You are a marvelous lover and you always, and I do mean always, leave me completely satisfied when we make love. You just can't do it as much as I need it."

"I'll tell you what Agnes (she hated to be called Agnes). I'll sign it if you make a few changes to it."

"What kind of changes?"

"You don't ever have sex with me on a day you have sex with others and we sleep in separate bedrooms."

"I can't do that. I need you and I need you in the bed with me. Why can't you get it through your thick skull that I love you and I don't want to lose you?"

"That's okay Agnes. Don't make the changes. I didn't want to sign your so called agreement anyway."

"All right! I'll make the damned changes and work on getting you back in bed with me later. I'll go to the computer, make the changes and be right back."

I tried to get off the chair, but the two guys forced me to sit there. I told them I had to go to the bathroom and one of them said:

"Just pee your pants. Miss Aggie said to keep you in the chair so you aren't getting up until she says so."

Aggie came back five minutes later, read the document to me and I said:

"Where do I sign?"

She held out a pen and I said, "Your two goons won't let me get up."

"Let him up guys."

I got up, walked over to her and set my briefcase down on the table and took the pen from her. Then I put the pen down and said:

"Not that I don't trust you, but I think I'll read it just to be sure that it says what you said it says."

I picked it up, read it and then I laughed and tore it up and threw it in her face. I picked up my briefcase and headed for the door.

"Stop him!" Aggie yelled and the two guys started after me and when they were close enough I spun around toward them with my briefcase heading for the first guy's head. It was a solid hit and he went down. The second guy was caught by surprise and before he realized it I was on him. I punched him in the mouth and he stumbled backwards and I kicked him in the balls as hard as I could and he went down, Being no dummy I knew that at two against one I needed to keep them down and I went to work giving the boot to both of them. I took turns kicking them in the crotch, ribs and head until Aggie screamed:

"Stop it Rob or I'll shoot you."

I looked over at Aggie and saw that she was pointing a gun at me.

"Go ahead and shoot you miserable cunt!"

I took out my cell phone, called 911, gave my name and address and told the operator that my wife was pointing a gun at me and threatening to shoot me. The operator told me to stay calm and do nothing that would excite my wife and that a car was on the way. I closed the phone and said:

"Thank you Agnes. The divorce will go a lot quicker and easier with you in jail."

"That was stupid Rob. When the police get here you will be the one arrested. You came in, found me talking to two friends, flew into a jealous rage and attacked them. It will be your word against ours. Three against one and we are fully clothed. You will be arrested for assault."

"Oh Agnes, how could you. There's all that love you have for me shining through."

"Don't sweat it Rob. I'll bail you out and Barry and Tony won't press charges. It will all work out."

"Think again Agnes. Hank saw these two bozos pick me up at work and Joyce next door saw them escort me into the house, My story is that you had me brought here against my will and when I attempted to leave you told your lovers to stop me and they tried and lost and then you pulled a gun on me. I may end up spending a night in jail, but when my witnesses speak their piece you will be the one sitting in jail and I damned sure won't be paying your bail.

"Let's see what we have here. Kidnapping. Unlawful detainment. I'm sure that there is some sort of charge for threatening me with the gun and lastly there will be knowingly making false statements to the police. There may even be others that I can't think of. Your best bet Agnes is to keep your mouth shut."

Aggie didn't take my advice and she and her two flunkies told their lies and I was taken to jail. In the morning I called Tom Sweet, told him what was going on and that he should get with Gaston Marshall, get the tapes and then do what had to be done. Aggie found out that she couldn't bail me out because I first had to go in front of a judge to get bail set and that wouldn't happen until Monday.

Tom had a friend who was an assistant district attorney and he played the tapes of what happened at the house for him. It showed Barry and Tony restraining me and Aggie pointing the gun at me and the ADA heard her say she was going to lie and have her two confederates lie. When Aggie showed up at the courthouse Monday morning for my bail hearing she was arrested. Warrants were sworn out for Barry and Tony and by nightfall they were under lock and key.

I refused to put up the bail for Aggie and her parents didn't have the money and couldn't get it. Aggie got an attorney and he called me and told me that a bail bondsman wanted me to put up the house as security for her bail bond and I laughed at him and hung up.

I moved out of the motel and back into the house and then called a locksmith and had all the locks changed. Because Aggie had threatened me with a gun Tom was able to get an order of protection against Aggie. If she did somehow manage to get out of jail she couldn't come within one thousand feet of me without being arrested and sent back to jail.

As good as Aggie's pussy might have been it apparently wasn't worth doing serious time over and both Barry and Tony gave up Aggie and took deals. Aggie said that she would never have pulled the trigger on me. She was just trying to get me to stop beating on her two cohorts before I killed one of them and had to go to jail for it.

The jury saw the tape and decided from some of the things she said, specifically her protestations of love for me, that she was probably telling the truth when she said she was only trying to stop me from killing Barry or Tony. They found her not guilty on the felony menacing charge, but did find her guilty of the unlawful restraint charges and the making a false police report charge and several other small charges.

The judge gave her nine months in the county jail and one thousand hours of community service when she was released from custody. While she was in jail the divorce skated through and all I lost on the deal, besides Aggie, was twenty percent of the equity in the house. I put the money in her account at the bank and then headed for the bar next to the motel I had stayed at.

I was in luck. Rhonda and Shelby were there and I asked them to celebrate my first day of freedom with me. Laura wasn't there because her hubby was home from the wars and they were busy getting reacquainted and playing catch up.

"So why do you want to celebrate with us?" Rhonda asked.

"Because I'm taking a shot in the dark here. I saw the rings on Laura and I can see the rings on Shelby, but you aren't wearing rings and I see no lines on your fingers that would indicate that you ever did have them so I am betting that there is no long haul trucker in your life. That and I've always had a thing for hot looking redheads."

Shelby laughed and said, "You are so busted girl" as I pulled Rhonda off her chair and led her out onto the dance floor.

End of the 1st Story

Momma's Boys

"Come on Yvonne, you know it ain't right."

"Oh stop your whining Dion. I can't help it that you were raised a prude. I wasn't and I'm not going to become one just to suit you."

"This ain't got nothing to do with being prudish Yvonne, it's got to do with decency."

"You calling me indecent Dion?"

"I'm just saying that it ain't right. The boys are at an age when things can get misunderstood."

"The boys can misunderstand what?"

"You know Vonnie, things."

"Things Dion?"

"Well yeah Vonnie, things."

Suddenly I knew what Dion was getting at and almost as suddenly I realized that he had a valid concern.

I am a forty-five year old woman with two grown and married daughters. My mother, my daughters, even my grandmother and aunts, along with myself, have never been ashamed of our bodies and we never worried about being scantily clad in front of the men in our family. I'm not talking nudity here; we just didn't spend a lot of time covering up around the house. My father, brothers, and an occasional uncle or two have seen me nude and it was no big thing. I grew up not being ashamed of my body and not thinking it wrong to see anyone else's. When I married at nineteen I lucked out and got a guy who was a free spirit and we eventually became nudists so I've never been overly concerned about clothes, especially in my own house.

I lost Don to cancer when I was thirty-nine and I mourned him for two years. Then I started dating and four years later I met and married Dion. Dion had two sons: Phillip who was nineteen and going on twenty, and Todd who had just turned eighteen. Almost from day one Dion was on me for the way I dressed around the house and I shrugged it off. That is I shrugged it off until I finally figured out what Dion's problem was - he was afraid of what might happen - he was jealous of his sons and he was afraid that they might see the way I ran around the house as a come on. Dion was afraid they might get lucky sometime when he was wasn't around!

To understand his concern you had to go back to that period in my life when I stopped mourning Don and started dating. There is no nice way of saying it; for those four years I was an absolute slut! The last year of Don's illness had been sexless and so had the two years I'd spent in widow's weeds. When I finally decided that it was time to get on with my life I went just a little overboard. I didn't mean to, but too much to drink one night had led to some multiple partner sex and I found that I liked it. I was never what you might call a gangbang queen; never did have sex with really large groups, but three or four was pretty common. It was during that period that I met Dion.

At first he didn't appear to be anyone special. He wasn't bad looking and he was a more than adequate lover, but he was just one of many. I didn't really pay much attention to him until I started noticing that he always seemed to be one of the three or four that I ended up in bed with. One morning, after one of my rare large groups - eight I think it was - I woke up and Dion was in bed with me. That was not a normal occurrence. Usually my sessions ended around three in the morning, everyone left, and I went to bed alone, but there was Dion in my bed at nine in the morning.

"What are you doing here?"

He reached over and began rolling my left nipple between his fingers and said, "Trying to make points."

My breasts are very sensitive and I moaned and said, "Well that's certainly one way of doing it."

After a little mutual head and a slow leisurely fuck Dion took me out to breakfast. Over coffee I asked, "So, what's the deal with trying to make points?"

"I'm trying to make points because I think that you would be a perfect fit for me."

"How's that?"

"Just that the perfect woman for me has to like sex as much as you seem to."

"Sorry sweetie, but I'm not looking for anything permanent."

"Maybe not now, but maybe someday. I just want to put my oar in early."

"Just out of curiosity explain to me how you see this prospective relationship."

"Open."

"Open? What's that mean?"

"Free to play as long as you come home."

"Both sides?"

"Of course. I'm not capable of being a one-woman man, but I do need a steady, stable relationship. The woman I have that relationship with will ideally feel the same way. I think that woman is you."

"Sorry sweetie, sounds good, but I'm nowhere near being ready for something like that."

"That's okay, I'm a patient man."

He was. We did start seeing more of each other and by the end of that four year period I was ready to cut back on my activities - not eliminate, but cut back - to once or twice a month and Dion was there to talk me into an open marriage.

Surprisingly, it worked. It was like a normal marriage except that when I felt the need for more than just one cock I was free to have them. Sometimes with Dion and sometimes without him and he had the same freedom if he found a lady he wanted to play with. Things were just fine until I figured out what Dion's problem was with the way I dressed around the house.

It was Dion's own fault. If he had just kept his mouth shut nothing would have changed, but once a slut, always a slut and I began to see my two step-sons as prime beef and a reason to never have to leave the house to play. I told Dion that I understood where he was coming from and that I would try and be a little more circumspect. And when he was home I was. When he wasn't home and either or both of the boys were, I turned into a tease. Actually I wasn't teasing; it was more along the lines of an open invitation. I left the bathroom door open when I was in the shower; I left the bedroom door open when I was dressing, I walked around the house in see-thru bra and panties and I smiled at the hard-ons I was producing. I did everything but flat out ask the boys to fuck me. I could tell that the boys were interested, but there were either too inexperienced or too scared to make a move. If it was going to happen, I was going to have to make it happen.

It was a Tuesday morning and Dion had just left for work. Todd had an early morning class so only Phillip and I were in the house. Phillip was still in bed and so I made my move. I stripped, put a touch of rouge on my nipples and walked into Phillip's bedroom. He was still asleep when I eased the covers off of him and I smiled when I saw that he slept naked. Not having to wrestle his PJs or boxers off was going to make it so much easier. I ran my tongue along the length of his soft cock, swirled it around his cockhead and then took him in my mouth. After that he was mine. He started to wake up and I was lying across his legs with my hot mouth sucking his rapidly hardening dick and by the time he was fully awake I was sliding my wet pussy down his stiff pole. I could see confusion and panic on his face and I leaned forward and whispered, "Relax baby, just relax and enjoy. Let mommy make you feel good. We have all day sweetie, all day and mommy wants to ring your chimes."

Phillip was not a virgin, but he wasn't all that experienced either. By four o'clock that afternoon, when I was finally able to pry myself away from his cock, he was a whole lot more experienced and eager to continue his education.

As I let his spent cock slip from my mouth I said, "This is our secret sweetie, right? If we keep this quiet we can do it again. Would you like that? Would you like some more of mommy's pussy?"

He grunted out a yes and reached up to pull me back down.

"Don't be a greedy guts sweetie. I have to get up and get dinner started. We wouldn't want daddy to come home and find you with your cock in me, would we? That would be a quick end to this and we don't want that, do we? Be a good boy, get up and get dressed and make your bed look a little less like a bed in a whore house and your horny step-mother will try and find a way to suck your cock before you go to bed tonight."

I was showered, sweet smelling and had dinner on the table when Dion got home. When he saw me he smiled and said, "You've been up to something, I can tell." I smiled back at him and told him that I had spent some quality time that afternoon with a rather horny young man.

"Anyone that I know?"

"No baby, just one of the guys I met on my last evening out."

"Did he leave enough for me?"

I giggled and told him that I thought I could fit him in. He went upstairs to get out of his dirty clothes and take a shower and as soon as I heard the shower running I hurried to the front room and started sucking Phillip's cock. I had one ear on the shower and the other listening for the front door as I slobbered all over Phillip's meat.

What I was hoping for was for Todd to come home and catch Phillip and me in the act while Dion was still in the shower, but it didn't happen. The shower stopped running just as Phillip came in my mouth and I was at the kitchen sink brushing my teeth when Todd finally got there.

It was two days before I had another chance to fuck Phillip, not that I hadn't been trying to get his cock sooner, but he felt he couldn't miss another day of classes. I couldn't catch a quickie before he left for school because Todd was always around.

I fully intended that Todd's cock was going to find its way into my pussy, but I either had to catch him alone as I had Phillip or let him catch Phillip and me in the act. I don't know why, but I just had the feeling that Phillip would balk if I suggested that we bring Todd in on the fun. I was actually so horny thinking of getting to fuck Phillip again that I had to go out bar hopping and get four guys to spend an afternoon with me in a motel.

Dion had just left for work and I was in the kitchen putting the dirty breakfast dishes in the dishwasher when Phillip walked into the room. I smiled at him and dropped the robe I was wearing to the floor. "Does this give you any ideas sweetie?" Phillip looked around nervously and I said, "What's the matter sweetie, don't want mommy anymore?"

"Todd is here."

"No he isn't sweetie. He left five minutes before your father did."

"Yeah, but he forgot a book and came back. He's upstairs right now."

"And you don't want to share mommy, is that it?"

"You said we had to keep it a secret."

"So I did sweetie, but what I meant was that we had to keep your father from finding out. So bring your cock over here to mommy and if Todd finds out and wants to join in I certainly won't object."

Phillip looked around, shrugged his shoulders and then he opened his fly and walked over to me. I was on my knees sucking his cock when I saw Todd standing in the doorway watching. I took my mouth off Phillip's cock and smiled at Todd, "Come on over here sweetie and let mommy show you how she likes to take care of her boys."

That was six months ago. I'm spending a lot more time at home these days although I still go out when I feel the need for more than two cocks. I know that Phillip and Todd could probably bring home a virile friend or three if I asked, but I'm a little leery of doing that. Young men tend to be quite boastful and the last thing I want is for it to get out that Phillip and Todd's mom is an easy lay. It might get back to Dion and while normally hearing that I'm getting fucked by other guys wouldn't bother him, the news that his sons are fucking his wife might.

My best days are the ones when Phillip and Todd are home all day while Dion is at work and then Dion comes home horny and keeps me busy all night. It is a shame that I can't figure out a way that I can have my three studs together because then I never would have to leave the house.

Who knows, one of these days I might get lucky, but until then I'll just have to be satisfied with "momma's boys" during the day and daddy at night.

End of the 2nd Story

Stephanie Anne

I met Stephanie Anne on my first day at college. We were attending freshman indoctrination and ended up sitting next to each other. I've never been shy and she was good looking so I immediately hit on her. We left indoctrination to go for a pizza and ended up back in my room where we practically ripped each other's clothes off. Steph had my cock in her mouth before I even got my T-shirt off. I hadn't been laid in months and she had me ready to cum in less than a minute and I told her I was going to shoot and all she did was grab my ass and pull my cock deeper into her mouth. I pushed her back on the bed and returned the favor until she screamed for me to fuck her and by the end of the night the roller coaster ride was on.

Steph was my twin, at least mentally and spiritually, and we had both come to college thinking more of the partying and good times than the studying. We spent more time in bed with each other than at the library or attending classes and I'm amazed at the fact that I was so surprised at finding out that I was flunking out. It was instantly, "Whoa up dude, dad is so going to kill you." It took a Herculean effort on my part, but I was able to pull my grades up enough to get me through the term. But the effort took me away from Steph more than she liked and so she dropped me and moved on.

I still saw her around the campus, usually with her lover of the moment, and I would feel pangs of longing. I dated a lot and I scored a lot, but no other girl ever made me feel like Steph had. About six months went by and one night there was a knock on my door and I opened it to find Steph standing there.

"May I come in?"

"Of course," I said as I stepped aside and let her by.

She looked around the place as if to see what changes might have been made since she left and I asked, "To what do I owe this unexpected visit?"

"I missed you."

And with those words we were off and running again.

It wasn't as hot and heavy as it had been the first time around because I had learned my lesson and studies now came first. It wasn't long before Steph got tired of not being at the top of my list and again we split. As what had happened after our first split I dated, I scored and I never found anyone to take Steph's place in my heart. Steph and I split up and got together two more times. Mutual friends kept me updated on Steph and what she was doing. Mostly it was party, party, party with a steady stream of lovers.

I could never figure it out. Steph seemed to learn by osmosis. It was like she walked by the library and everything inside just flowed out through the air and into her mind. The woman never, at least that I saw, studied a lick, yet she maintained a solid B average. Near the end of my junior year Steph showed up on my doorstep again.

"Like a bad penny I just keep turning up. I can't seem to stay away from you sweetie."

That time we lasted almost six months. The pressures during the middle of my senior year caused me to spend almost no time on Steph and suddenly she was gone again. With graduation fast approaching I didn't have much time to mourn the fact that she was gone again other than to reflect that it was probably for good that time as graduation would be followed by my leaving town.

Graduation out of the way and sheepskin in hand I set out to find a job and start my new life.

***

I found a good job, met a lovely lady named Christine and married her and three years later I divorced her. She was supposed to be working late on a big project that was coming up on a deadline and I decided to surprise her at work. I stopped for some take out so we could have dinner together and then I'd leave her to finish her work and go on home. I walked into her office and found her on her back on her desk while some guy she worked with was between her legs and putting it to her. I was very civilized about it. I walked over to her desk and set the take out down next to her head:

"Here, you two might need this to keep up your strength," I said as I turned and walked away.

Six months went by, the divorce became final, and one evening I came home from work to find Steph sitting on my doorstep waiting for me. She stood up, threw her arms around me, gave me a kiss that left me weak in the knees and said:

"The grapevine says you are single now, true?"

"It is indeed."

"Good! I've waited long enough. Show me your bedroom."

"What do you mean you have waited long enough?"

"I mean I knew in college that you were meant to be my life partner, but I just wasn't ready to settle down yet. I always knew that you would be there for me to come back to and then suddenly you weren't. It killed me when you graduated and left without even coming to see me to say goodbye. I wouldn't have let you go, but you didn't give me the chance. By the time I found you, you were married. I knew it wouldn't last so I kept track of you and now she's gone and here I am."

"What do you mean you knew it wasn't going to last?"

"She started running around on you six months after you got married. I knew you would eventually catch her and so I waited. I gave you six months to get over it. Now come on sweetie, where's your bedroom?"

***

The old magic was there and three weeks later Steph moved in with me. Six months went by and one evening after Steph had destroyed me in bed she asked me when I was going to make an honest woman out of her. I didn't know what to say. My college relationship with Steph and my marriage to Christine had me leery of relationships. I didn't doubt that Steph had strong feelings for me and I knew how I felt about her, but I also remembered all the times she walked away from me. True, she came back, but it was the times she left that I remembered. Steph saw the hesitation and said:

"Don't panic sweetie, I've waited this long and I can wait until you are ready. I'll wait as long as it takes."

She never mentioned it again, but I always knew that it was never far from her mind.

Another year went by and Steph was still with me and we were getting along great together. In fact, my time with Steph was much better than my time had been over the same length of time with Christine and I thought my life with Christine had been perfect. So I sucked it up and I asked Steph to marry me. We were married in a civil ceremony. Three great years went by before I could finally give Steph the honeymoon I promised. I finally had enough money in the bank and enough time off coming to me so we packed our bags and flew down to San Juan, Puerto Rico.

***

We spent eight days lying on the beach, soaking up sun, swimming in the ocean and enjoying the nightlife. Steph is a good looking woman and one of the truisms of life is that good looking women attract the male of the species and if you have a good looking woman you had to learn to live with the constant attention she got and learn to handle it. If Steph went somewhere alone or if I left her alone she got hit on. It was a fact of life. I didn't have to like it, but I did have to live with it.

I was sitting in a beach chair nursing a Pina Colada and watching Steph wade in the surf. A man waded up to her and started talking with her and a couple of minutes later another man joined them. I saw Steph smile and laugh at something one of the men said and then she said something and the two men smiled and a minute or so later they walked away. I wrote it off as two guys hitting on her and her gently shooting them down.

The hot sun and the Pina Colandas did a number on me and I napped a while. I opened my eyes a couple of times and once I thought I saw Steph sitting and talking with the man who had approached her when she was wading in the surf. After an hour or so I shook myself awake and found Steph sitting in the chair next to me. I told her I was going up to the room to get out of the sun for a while and she told me to run along and that she would be up later. I could see the beach from in front of the elevators and just before getting on I saw the man Steph had been talking to sit down next to her in the chair I had just vacated.

An hour later Steph came up to the room and we dressed for dinner. I didn't know if it was something I ate, too much sun, too many Pina Coladas or a combination of all three, but suddenly I didn't feel all that great and I wanted to go back to the room. Steph told me to go on ahead, but that she wanted to take a walk on the beach.

"It's a full moon tonight sweetie and I might never again have the chance to see the beach and the ocean under a full moon."

I told her to enjoy herself and I headed for the room. On my way to the elevator I noticed the man that Steph had been talking to sitting alone at the bar off the lobby. I was just reaching to push the UP button when suddenly I had a very bad feeling. I had no idea why, but I knew that something was wrong and I just knew that it concerned Steph and that man. I left the elevator and moved across the lobby to where I could sit behind some potted palms and see the man at the bar.

Less than five minutes after I sat down Steph went into the bar and slid onto the stool next to the man. They sat and talked and two drinks later the man put his arm around Steph and she didn't shrug it off or push it away. Another minute and they leaned toward each other and kissed. Two minutes later they got up and, hand in hand, they left the bar. I got up and followed them. Had they been a little less wrapped up in each other they couldn't have failed to spot me behind them, but it seemed that no one else existed for them.

Apparently the man had some bucks because he walked Steph to one of the first floor suites that had a patio that let right out onto the beach and they didn't come cheap. He slid his key card through the slot and opened the door and I was just about to holler out:

"Hey asshole, just what do you think you doing with my wife?" when I realized just how stupid that would sound. He knew what he was doing with my wife and what's more, Steph knew it too. The door closed behind them and the 'click' of the door lock signaled the end of my marriage to Steph.

I turned and started for my room, but 'denial' set in before I had gone two steps.

Maybe it was something innocent like maybe they were friends – someone Steph knew before we got married and they were just going to talk and catch up on what had been happening in each other's lives. Maybe Steph just wanted some company because I didn't feel well and she didn't want... and so on. I convinced myself that I had to know for sure before I just walked away. But how? Then I remembered that the first floor rooms on that side of the hotel had patios just off the beach. I counted off the number of rooms to the lobby and then I went outside and counted backward until I got to what I thought was the patio to the room that Steph had gone into.

I quietly moved up to the patio door and looked in. The sliding glass door was closed, but the drapes were open. I looked in and saw a simply ravishing redhead bouncing up and down on a cock as she watched a room service waiter undress. When he was naked he approached the couple on the bed and presented his stiff cock to the redhead's mouth and she smiled at him and then swallowed the head. Wrong room! Wrong room, but I didn't want to leave. I wanted to stay there and watch, but as much as I wanted to I knew I had to move on. I needed, desperately needed, to know what Steph was doing. I reluctantly pulled myself away from the porn show and moved to the next patio.

The glass door was open, but the drapes were closed and I carefully pulled one side open just enough to let me see into the room. I would have been happier had I stayed and watched the redhead. Steph and the man were kissing and slowly undressing each other. To their right on the couch the second man who had approached Steph while she was in the surf that morning sat naked and stroking his cock.

"Any problems?" the sitting man asked.

"No. The stuff you gave Stephie to slip in his food made him sick just like you said it would. He is probably upstairs with his head in the toilet. What about you Stephie love, where is your head going to be?"

"As if you didn't know," Steph said as she slid to her knees in front of him and took hold of his cock. "I've missed this guy Brian. There hasn't been a day since school I haven't thought about it."

"What's the matter, hubby can't hack it in bed?"

"Hubby does just fine in bed thank you and I love him to death, but he can't light me up the way you always have."

"Bullshit Stephie, it isn't me and you know it. It is what I bring to the party. How many do you want tonight?"

"As many as I can get in three hours. After that I need to get back up to my hubby."

Brian nodded to the man on the couch and he picked up the phone and punched in a number. When the phone was answered all he said was, "We're ready" and he hung up the phone. Brian pulled his cock out of Steph's mouth, turned her toward the man on the couch and she dutifully walked over to him, bent at the waist and took his cock in her mouth. Brian moved up behind her, nudged her legs apart and then entered her from behind and started fucking her. Two minutes later there was a knock on the door and Brian pulled out of Steph long enough to walk over to the door and let three men, one of them black, into the room.   After that it was just a fuck-a-thon as the five men took turns using Steph as a cum dump.

And Steph loved it. She moaned, she screamed, she clutched, grabbed and spewed some of the foulest language I'd ever heard come from her mouth. I'd never heard Steph beg to be fucked in her ass, let alone heard her call it her poop chute, her dirt road, her Hershey Highway. I'd never heard her use the words cunt, snatch or fuck hole. She cried out for them to give her their splooge, their dick snot, their jizz and their junk. She pleaded with all of them to get her pregnant (even though her tubes had been tied), knock her up and give her a fat belly. She was especially hot for the black guy to get her pregnant.

"Imagine my hubby's face when a black baby pops out. Come on baby, you can do it. Flood me with your black baby making seed, drown my eggs and give me twins, triplets even. Come on lover, cuckold my white husband."

Steph took them on two and three at a time. She was on her knees with a cock in her mouth and one in her ass when Brian said:

"Hurry up and finish guys. We have to get the lady back to her husband."

The two finished and Steph dressed and Brian handed her an envelope. "Just a little in his food every day will keep him too sick to want to make love. Just keep dosing his food until you think your holes are closed up enough."

While Steph was dropping the envelope in her purse, I saw the black man dump something in a drink and mix it up until it dissolved. He walked over to Steph, handed her the drink and said:

"Here, drink this. Swish it around in your mouth a few times before you swallow it so it will wash the taste of cock and cum out of your mouth. Wouldn't want hubby to notice anything when you kiss him."

"Thanks," Steph said as she took the drink and did as the man had suggested.

I headed for the lobby to confront Steph as she came out of the room, but was slow in getting there. I got into the lobby just in time to see Steph stagger and the black man catch her before she could fall. She looked glassy eyed and suddenly I understood. The black man hadn't given Steph something to kill the taste of cum in her mouth – he had drugged her. I watched as he walked her out the front door and then waved. Seconds later a car pulled up and the man pushed Steph into the back seat.

I stood there, confused by the sudden turn of events, but I suddenly snapped out of my confused state. I didn't give a rat's ass what was going to happen to Steph, but I didn't want any of it coming back on me so I rushed to the door in time to get the license plate number of the car before it drove off. Then I went up to the room and went to bed.

***

The next day I got up and noticed that Steph wasn't there and shrugged my shoulders 'so what'. I went down to the beach and stretched out to soak up some sun. About an hour later someone put a blanket down beside me and I looked over and saw that it was the ravishing redhead. She smiled at me:

"Mind if I squat down here beside you?"

"Not at all."

"I didn't think you would. Where did you go last night?"

"What?"

"You left before it got interesting. I had the room service waiter call a couple of friends."

I was busted so I just smiled and said, "I had to leave before I kicked down the door to get in and join you."

"Too bad you didn't. I might not have had to have the waiter call for reinforcements. Do you often peep in windows?"

"No, but when you leave the lights on and don't close the drapes you can be seen from the beach and there aren't many men that I know who would pass up a show like that."

"You don't lie well sweetie. You were looking in the wrong room, weren't you? You meant to look in the one next to mine."

"How did you know?"

"I was seeing my herd out the door when your wife and her herd came out of the room. And where is your wife today?"

"She ran off with some black dude."

"You don't seem to be too worried about it."

"I'm not."

"You one of those couples that have an arrangement?"

"No. She decided to cheat and she got caught. When she gets back I'll let her know she's history and I'll move on" and then I explained the situation to her.

"Poor baby. Need some comforting?"

"What do you mean?"

"It's my last day here and I want to make the most of it. Want to play?"

"I don't think so. Not that I wouldn't love to, but I remember something that my first grade teacher wrote on one of my report cards. She noticed that I didn't play well with others."

She looked at me confused and then it dawned on her, "Oh no sweetie, it will be just you and me. I only do what I did last night once in a great while."

"Why do it at all?"

"You're a man sweetie and you wouldn't understand, but there is absolutely nothing in the world as satisfying to a woman as a good gangbang. I did them all the time in college, but I had to put them behind me when I got married."

"You are married?"

"Oh yes, and very happily too."

"I don't understand. How can you be happily married and do what you did last night?"

"I have a very understanding husband. Once every two years he lets me take a week's vacation by myself, no questions asked. He knows what I'm doing, but he also knows that I'm crazy about him and that I'll always come home to him. So, one week every two years I go off by myself and get all the wildness out of my system. It works for us. So, you going to help me on my last day?"

After what Steph had done there wasn't any use in my being faithful so I smiled and said:

"How could I possibly refuse a lovely lady's request?"

***

She loved to fuck. She loved taking it up the butt, she loved to suck cock and she was insatiable. She flat wore me out and I fell asleep in her bed. She woke me up in the morning with a blow job and when she had me as hard as a steel I-beam she asked me to do her one more time in her ass.

"I love it and it is the one thing that my husband will not do so it will be two years before I can do it again."

She got the lube we had used earlier out of her travel case and handed it to me and then she got on the bed on her knees and buried her head in a pillow. I lubed up my fingers and thumb and began to work on her anal rosebud to loosen it up and to prepare it for my cock and when she felt she was ready she told me to go ahead.

"Easy baby, nice and easy, slow and gentle until I warm up."

I slid slowly into her and felt her anal walls grip my cock like a tight fist. "That feels so good" she moaned, "A little harder honey and just a little faster. God honey, you feel so hard. Fuck me honey, fuck me."

I gripped her hips and slammed my cock into her for several

minutes as she moaned, "Yes yes yes yes, like that honey, just like that." And then she cried out, "Don't stop baby, don't stop, I'm almost there, I'm close, I'm close, OH GOD!" and I felt her body tremble and seconds later I sent my load into her butt.

As I was dressing to leave she asked, "Did you enjoy yourself?"

"Silly question, you know I loved every minute of it."

"Did you enjoy yourself enough that I can ask you for a favor?"

"What?"

"At least talk to your wife before you walk away from her. She might be just like me. She may love you dearly, but need to get rid of the wildness every now and then. At least talk to her, okay?"

I remembered that Steph had said she loved me to death before she started her gangbang so I said that I would think about it, we kissed goodbye and I went up to my room.

***

Steph wasn't there and there was no sign that she had returned while I was gone so I called the police and reported her missing. I told them that we had gotten into an argument and she had stormed out of the room and gone down to the bar. I told them that after about a minute or so I had gone down after her and saw her getting into a car and drive off. I gave them the plate number of the car and then I went to breakfast.

I spent the rest of the day on the beach or swimming in the ocean and that evening after dinner I started packing. I packed all of Steph's stuff and was debating whether to leave it with the hotel or give it the police to hold when the phone rang. It was the police and would I please come down to the lobby. The call decided me so I took Steph's bags with me when I went down.

"We found your wife. She's in pretty bad shape and we took her to the hospital."

"By bad shape you mean what? Severally beaten, bones broken?"

"No. We found her at a private residence and she was being sexually abused. It appears that she was drugged and was being used as a sexual plaything by a large number of men."

"So what do you need from me?"

The officer looked surprised at the comment and said, "We are here to take you to the hospital."

"No thanks, but here" and I handed him Steph's two bags. "Her clothing and return ticket are in the bags. Since you are going to the hospital anyway would you see that she gets them?"

"You aren't going to see her?"

"No I'm not. I've thought about it a lot since I called you. She didn't have enough time to go into the bar and pick up somebody in the time between storming out of the room and my following her downstairs. That means that the argument with me was a set up and she had someone waiting down in the lobby for her to come down. She didn't expect me to follow her and see what she was up to. Whoever it was that she met is who she got in the car with. Whatever happened to her was of her own making and as far as I'm concerned she has made her bed and now she can lie in it."

I went back to the room, finished packing, left a wake up call for six and went to bed. At midnight the phone rang and it was Steph. I hung up on her and the phone immediately rang again. Again it was Steph and again I hung upon her and then I left the phone off the hook. Because the phone was off the hook I never got my six o'clock wake up, but it didn't matter because I didn't sleep for shit anyway.

***

I spent the flight home trying to read a book without making a whole lot of progress. I kept thinking about Steph and what she had done. I thought about all the times she had walked away from me in college and I wondered if each time she had gone to Brian – the man whose cock she had thought about every day since leaving school. I thought about what Marcie (the redhead) had said, about the need to let the wildness out every once in a while. Is that what Steph had done? Or was it something that Steph had been doing all along and I just hadn't found out about it.

The phone was ringing when I walked in to the house. Caller ID showed the Puerto Rico area code so I ignored it. The answering machine clicked on, but then clicked right back off which meant that it was full. I played some of them and found that they were all calls from Steph begging me to pick up. I deleted all the messages and went upstairs to unpack. The phone rang again and again caller ID showed the call coming from San Juan. I was just going to let it ring, but then I decided that I needed to get it over with:

"Hello?"

"Oh thank God, at last! Where have you been? Why haven't you been taking my calls?"

"Why would I want to talk to a gangbang whore Stephanie?"

"Baby, you don't understand. I was drugged, I didn't know what was happening."

I was all set to bring up what I saw, but then decided that I wanted to be looking her in the eye when I did it. "What do you want Stephanie?"

"I want to come home."

"Your ticket is in your suitcase."

"Will you pick me up at the airport?"

"No."

"I don't have any money. How will I get home?"

"That's up to you Stephanie" and I hung up on her.

***

The next day was my first day back to work and after work I stopped with a few of the guys to have a beer. It was almost nine when I got home. The lights were on so I guessed that Steph had managed to get home after all. As soon as I walked in the door I got:

"Where the hell have you been?"

"Having drinks with the guys after work. Told them all about what a smashing good time I had in San Juan."

"You don't seem like you were worried about me at all."

"I wasn't."

"Don't you even care about what happened to me?"

"No, why should I. You brought it on yourself."

"How can you say that? I was drugged and taken against my will."

"Yeah, right!"

"What do you mean by that?"

"It means I don't believe you."

"I can prove it damn you, I've got the toxicology report from the hospital."

"Okay Steph, just when and how were you drugged?"

"It was when I finished my walk on the beach. I stopped at the bar for a drink and the guy sitting next to me slipped something in my drink when I got up to go to the bathroom. God, it was horrible. For two days I was raped by one man after another and only God knows how much longer it would have gone on had the police not raided the place."

"That's your story and you're sticking to it?"

"Yes."

"See? I told you that you were lying to me."

"Damn it, what is wrong with you. I'm your wife for God's sake and I've just been through hell and you don't seem to care."

"I don't care Steph. You see Stephanie, I know a hell of a lot more than you think I do. I was still in the lobby when you went into the bar and joined your old college chum, you know, the one whose cock you've thought about every day since you left school? I watched you go to his room. I was outside on the patio when you did your little three-hour gangbang. You were drugged by that black asshole who gave you the drink and told you to swish it around in your mouth to get rid of the cock and cum taste in case I wanted to kiss you. If I hadn't gotten the plate number of the car you drove off in and given it to the cops you would still be over there on your back doing what you seem to like to do. So you see Stephanie, you did it to yourself and I'll be damned if I'm going to feel sorry for you."

Her face was pale as she stared at me and in a low quavering voice she said:

"It's not what you think Paul. I know it looks bad, but it isn't what you think. I can explain Paul, can we at least talk about it?"

"No Stephanie, we can't talk about it. Maybe someday when I'm not mad enough to kill we can talk about it, but not now. I've moved all of your stuff into the spare bedroom. You'll stay there until I figure out what I'm going to do."

"Going to do? What does that mean?"

"Just what I said Stephanie. Kick you out, divorce you, talk to you, decide if anything can be saved from this mess – until I figure out what to do."

***

For the next three weeks Steph would look at me expectantly when I came home from work, but I went out of my way to ignore her. She would have dinner ready and waiting, but the meals would be silent and when they were over I would get up and go into my home office or down into my basement workshop. At the end of three weeks I finally felt like I could talk with Steph without losing it so one night I came home and at dinner I told her that I was ready to talk.

"But no bullshit Steph, and no lies. If I hear either it is over. Do I make myself clear?"

The story Steph told me pretty much mirrored the story Marcie told me about herself. Steph had gotten involved with Brian the first time we had split and he had gotten her high on pot and beer one night and she had gotten gangbanged and she had loved it. She loved it, but she knew it was destructive behavior and she swore never to do it again, but it always seemed that when she split from me that Brian was there waiting and she would end up doing it again.

"Honest to God Baby, I put it all behind me when we got married. No man has touched me since we got married, at least not until San Juan. It was just pure bad luck that Brian was there when we got there. Bad luck that he was there and that I was weak. I hadn't done it since college, but I always thought about it. I always remembered how it made me feel. Brian worked on me for five days before I finally gave in.

"It had nothing at all to do with my loving you Paul, nothing at all. I love you Paul, I always have. You are my life partner, we were always meant to be together. I'll do anything to make it up to you baby. I'll do anything to atone for being stupid and for doing what I did. Please honey, just give me a chance."

"I suppose that I have my own self to blame. By taking you back every time you left I guess I showed you that it would be okay to shit on me, that I would put up with it, but this time you really shit on me big time Stephanie."

"Give me a chance. Please honey, please let me try and make it up to you."

***

Well, I gave her a chance and I'd like to be able to say that we survived, but we didn't and it was my fault, not hers. She did everything she could think of to show me that she loved me and the stupid thing is that I know she did, or for that matter still does. No, the problem was me. I just could not get past one of the things she had done. I could never get past the fact that she had drugged my food to get me out of the way. Steph didn't have a medical background and she had no idea of what it was that Brian had given her to use on me. It was just:

"Here, put this in his food and it will get him out of the way."

It could have been LSD, it could have been rat poison or it could have been anything in between and she just took it and slipped it to me. And she was going to do it again to keep me sick until her 'looseness' went away. I just could not get by that.

Steph begged me not to divorce her and so I haven't, but we don't live together anymore although she does call me every day. She is still clinging to the hope that I'll give in and take her back like I always have before and who knows, it could happen. It isn't likely, but it could happen.

End of the 3rd Story

Merrily The Maid

Merrily tells me that it is not incest, but I can't help but believe that it is. Not that I'm going to stop, mind you but I do sometimes wonder about what her mother would say.

Mary and I had been together almost thirty years when she passed on. She was my third and I was her second and both of us were leery of marriage and so we lived together for seven years before we made it legal. All of my kids went with my ex-wives and after my last child with the second wife I had a vasectomy so Mary and I never had kids of our own. But Mary brought two kids from her first marriage with her and I helped raise them as if they were my own. They grew up, married and started raising children of their own, but we remained close.

***

I was sixty when cancer took Mary. I sold the house, bought a small condo and tried to get on with my life. One of the first things that I did was hire Merry Maids to come in and clean for me. When Merrily, my stepdaughter, heard about that she went ballistic. I was wasting my money paying someone to come in and do what Merrily would do for free. But I was alone for the first time in my life and as much as I missed Mary I kind of liked it and I felt that Merrily being around would somehow take that away from me. That was the other thing that upset Merrily - my being alone. She set out on a campaign to get rid of Merry Maids and to get someone into my life.

I resisted on the Merry Maids, but eventually I got tired of arguing with Merrily over it and I let them go. Merrily started coming over twice a week and doing the cleaning. I did my own dishes and did my own laundry and in general picked up after myself, but Merrily did the rest. I fought her tooth and nail on her campaign to find someone for me. She was forever inviting me over to dinner and when I got there she would have another dinner guest to introduce me to. A simple picnic in the park with her and the grandchildren would bring something like, "Oh, look who's here. Dad, I'd like you to meet…" It got so I wouldn't accept any more invitations from her but that didn't stop her. Once the grandkids wanted to spend the weekend with me, but did Merrily bring them over? No, she sent them over with someone she wanted me to meet.

I finally lost it and told her that if she did it to me again I would embarrass whoever the person was so bad that the person would never speak to Merrily again.

"But dad, mom wouldn't want you to sit home alone. She'd kill me if she knew I wasn't trying to help you."

"You can help me best by letting me live my life like I want to."

Merrily finally realized that she wasn't going to win that one so she took her Merry Maids victory, settled for half a loaf and stopped playing cupid.

***

I was retired and had a lot of free time on my hands and one day I sat down at the computer and decided to see what all this Internet fuss was about and the more I played with it the more I found and I became a Net Junkie. More specifically - I became a Net porn junkie and in no time at all I had over twenty sites under "favorites" on the computer. Those sites were my sex life and on any given day I would visit them and masturbate to get sexual relief. The question could be asked, "Why didn't you hook up with the women that Merrily was trying to set you up with rather than use your hand?" The answer was simple. Merrily was trying to set me up with women my own age and while they were all very nice ladies they looked like what they were - sixty year old grandmothers and great grandmothers. While they might have been comfortable living with they had zero sex appeal. It is one of the sad facts of life that even though you are in your sixties your mind still thinks like that of a thirty-five year old and the women you lust after are the women you lusted after when you were that age. But those women have as much interest in you as you have for the women your own age. So anyway, I was able to satisfy my sexual urges by hand after being stimulated by the porn ladies I could never have.

***

Merrily had no set schedule for coming over to clean the house. It averaged twice a week and when she was there I sometimes hardly knew it. She had her own key and would come and go and sometimes I only knew that she had been there because she would leave me a list of things that I needed to buy before she came back the next time. I was sitting at the computer, cock in hand, and watching a home clip of a woman doing her husband and his best friend when I heard, "Oh my" and I looked over to see Merrily standing in the doorway - I hadn't heard her come in. It was one of those moments when time seemed to stop. I sat there staring at her open mouthed and with cock in hand and she stood there staring back at me. I'm sure it was only a fraction of a second, but it seemed like forever.

Before I understood what was happening Merrily stepped forward saying, "You shouldn't be doing that" and she went to her knees next to me while pushing my hand away from my cock. She took it in her hand and began stroking it as she said, "I tried to get you someone to do this for you." She stroked it one or two more times and then she said, "Oh shit" and she bent and took my cock in her mouth.

Honest to God I tried to tell myself to push her away, that I'd raised her, that she was my stepdaughter and I shouldn't let - no, couldn't - let it happen, but it had been over three years since a hot mouth had bobbed up and down on my cock. I couldn't even bring myself to tell her I was going to cum and it caught her completely unaware. Merrily's head jerked up for a second and then went back down and swallowed what she could. My cock started to go soft and I expected Merrily to get up and run from the room. For a moment she was motionless, as if she were trying to think of a way to exit gracefully and then her hand cupped my balls and she started sucking me again.

It took her awhile. At my age you don't recover all that quickly, but eventually my cock began to get stiff again. When it was hard she stood up and dropped her shorts and underpants. I started to stand up but she put a hand on my shoulder and told me to stay put. Her hot mouth wasn't on my cock anymore and I was thinking a little more clearly. I opened my mouth to say, "We can't" but she put her hand over my mouth and then she straddled me and sat down. My cock split her pussy lips and she shoved herself down on me until I was in as far as our bodies would permit. Her head was on my shoulder and she said, "Don't say a word, just fuck me."

For minutes it was a slow and leisurely up and down, but then she began to moan and the tempo picked up and finally she got off me and pulled me down to the floor. Her legs spread wide and she cried, "Hurry" and then I was fucking her as hard as I could.

She planted both feet on the floor and pushed herself up at me, her nails dug into my ass and she whined, "Please please please" and then her body shook and her legs locked behind mine and her feet were drumming on the back of my legs. My heart was beating like a jackhammer and my breath was becoming ragged and Merrily was mewling, "Don't stop, don't stop, don't stop" and then she hit the peak of her orgasm. I came in her and the fell exhausted to the floor beside her. I lay there gasping for breath and Merrily sat up and looked down at me, "Are you all right?"

"Just out of breath. It's been a long time."

She grinned at me, "Well you're not through yet old man" and she stood up and offered me her hand. I took it and she helped me up and then led me to the bedroom. As she pulled me along I was babbling, "We can't do this, we shouldn't, it's not right" and all the other arguments against committing incest that I could think of. She ignored me and when we got to the bedroom she pushed me back on the bed, lay down beside me and started to play with my limp dick.

"In the first place it is not incest, at least not in so far as I understand the definition. You are not my father. Granted, you have been a thousand times more fatherly to me than the asshole that got my mother pregnant, but you are not my biological father."

"That doesn't matter. I raised you as my own so for all practical purposes you are my daughter."

"I don't care. You did a hell of a lot more for me than my real father ever did and now I get to do something for you."

I started to say something and Merrily put her hand over my mouth, "Shut up dad, just relax and enjoy."

It was another two hours before Merrily got around to picking up her shorts and panties and then she wanted to sit down and talk.

"Why won't you let me fix you up with someone?"

I explained to her the sixties body and thirty-five mind thing and she thought about it for a minute. "So, if I can find you a sexy forty year old with a thing for older men you would go for it?"

"Yes, I probably would, but I can already tell you it isn't going to happen."

"Why not, I'm thirty-eight and I just had a grand time with a sixty year old man."

"Yeah, well, this was a rather strange circumstance."

"Okay, I accept the challenge. I will find you a sexy younger woman. It might take me a while, but until I do you will just have to settle for me."

I started to protest and Merrily held up her hand, "Don't say it.

It's not your choice, it's mine." She looked around; "This place is in worse shape than I thought. I may have to come over three or four times a week instead of just two."

End of the 4th Story

New Slut In Town

My wife is the sweetest, most likeable woman in the world. She teaches Sunday school, teaches bible classes two nights a week and volunteers to work for every worthwhile charity in town and the strongest cuss word I've ever heard her utter is 'darn'. She is a great mother to our kids and has been a fabulous wife for me and I'm not kidding when I say that Marlene has absolutely no faults as a person. But not everyone sees her the same way I do. You see, Marlene has a problem - she looks like a slut.

It's really not her fault and outside of never leaving the inside of our house there doesn't seem to be anything she can do about it. It doesn't matter how she wears her hair, what style of clothes or make up she wears she still looks like and gives off the aura of a slut. She looked like a slut in her wedding dress, she looked like a slut in her maternity clothes, and when her father died and she went to his funeral in basic black and wearing a veil she still looked like a slut.

In all honesty the slutty look is one of the reasons that I started dating Marlene. I thought she was a slut and I was going to get an easy piece of ass, but I was soon disabused of that notion in the form of a ringing slap across my face on our second date. It only took the two dates to show me what kind of person that she really was and by then I was hooked - hooked on and fascinated by the contrast between the person she was and the person she looked like. The slutty look is a major turn on for me and fortunately Marlene is an absolute slut in our bed. She loves sex and will anything at least once to see if it rings our chimes. Anal, oral, mild domination, she even tried (and absolutely did not like) watersports once just to see what it would be like. But she is only slutty when she is in our bedroom with me.

Unfortunately her slutty look is a major turn on for almost all the other guys too. She is constantly being hit on and it is something that I have learned to live with. I used to get all bent out of shape when guys put the move on her and many are the times when she stopped me from going after some guy:

"Honestly dear, you have no need to act like that. I am perfectly capable of handling these situations on my own."

Eventually I stopped worrying about her and that proved to be a very big mistake.

***

It was a Christmas party at the home of Ron and Betty; a couple we were good friends with. We knew about half the people there, but the other half were friends of theirs that we had never met. We circulated and met new people, visited with old friends and in general had a good time. About an hour into the party Marlene went into the kitchen to help Betty with something and Ron and I started talking football with two other guys. About an hour or so later I went looking for Marlene, but I couldn't find her anywhere. I asked Betty if she'd seen her and Betty looked away from me and with a strange look on her face said she hadn't seen Marlene for quite a bit.

I kept looking and about fifteen minutes later Ron came up to me and said:

"What's the matter? You look like you lost something."

I told him I couldn't find Marlene and I asked him if he'd seen her. He got a look on his face that I could only classify as 'guilty' and said he hadn't seen her and then he hurried away to talk to someone else. Another half an hour went by and still no Marlene so I went to Betty and told her I needed to use the phone.

"Marlene is gone and that is not at all like her. I'm going to call the police."

Alarm came over Betty's face and she said, "No! Please don't do that. Please, it will only cause trouble."

I looked at her, "You had better explain that," I said.

Betty's face showed that she was worried and then she said, "Marlene is upstairs in the master bedroom."

I was silent for a moment and then I asked, "Why didn't you tell me that earlier?"

Betty looked down at the floor and said in a voice that was almost a whisper, "She's not alone."

I looked at her like she was crazy, "What are you trying to say?"

She said, "I'm sorry. I like Marlene a lot, but I couldn't help it. I had to keep quiet for Ron's sake."

And then the story came out. Ron's boss Harry was at the party and he took one look at Marlene and said, "Anybody that looks that slutty has got to be one hell of a great piece of ass. Before the night's over I'm going to nail her."

Ron tried to tell Harry that Marlene wasn't that way, but his boss said, "Before the night is over she will be." Ron was afraid to buck his boss because it could have cost him his job so when he saw Harry do something to Marlene's drink Ron had pretended that he had seen nothing and turned his back and walked away. And when his boss had maneuvered Marlene upstairs Ron had been talking to me to keep my back turned to the stairs.

"He's been up there with her for over an hour and a half?"

Again Betty looked down at the floor, "He and a few others."

I turned from her and headed for the stairs and by the time I got to the top of the stairs Betty was right behind me. She grabbed my arm:

"Please don't make a scene. Ron needs this job. He will never find another one like it that pays this well. It's too late to do anything about it now. Leave it be, please? I'll do anything you want. You can fuck me, I'll suck your cock, you can fuck my ass, you can have me as much and as often as you like, but please don't make a scene."

I pulled away from her and walked to the master bedroom and opened the door and then froze in my tracks. It had been my intention to go into the room kicking ass and taking names. I knew that I'd come out the loser if there were more than two in the room with her, but damn it, it was my wife in there! But when the door opened the scene that met my eyes changed all that. Marlene was naked and on her hands and knees. Her face was in the lap of the man sitting on the bed and his hands were on her head as it bobbed up and down on his cock. I couldn't tell whether his hands were resting on her head or if he was moving her head up and down. Behind her another man was sliding his cock into her and again I couldn't tell if she was pushing her ass back at the man or whether his hands on her hips doing it.

There were three other guys in the room and they were all watching what was going on and stroking their erections. I watched as the man sitting on the bed said, "Here it comes honey" and I saw cum dribble out of the corners of her mouth. When he got up and his cock was no longer in her mouth I heard Marlene's voice:

"Oh god that feels so good. Fuck me baby, fuck me."

Another man slid onto the bed and her mouth went straight for his cock.

"See? She likes it," I heard Betty whisper in my ear. "She's having a good time. Don't spoil it for her. Come on; let me take your mind off of it" and she tugged me backwards, away from the door and then reached around me to quietly close it. She turned me around, put her arms around me and kissed me. Her tongue was in my mouth and without breaking loose from me she walked us backward to the bedroom across the hall.

"I'll take your mind off her baby. I'm a real slut and I love to fuck. If you and Marlene hadn't come tonight that would be me over there and I'd be loving it."

While she talked, she undressed me and when she had me naked she went to her knees and took my cock in her mouth. I'd always thought Marlene was a good cocksucker, but Betty could have given Marlene lessons. While she sucked me off she was undressing herself and by the time she had her clothes off she had me ready to cum. I told her so and her reaction was to grab the cheeks of my ass and pull my cock deep into her throat. I blasted my load into her mouth and she gulped and gulped and swallowed it all. She got up and took hold of my limp dick and led me to the bed:

"Don't worry baby. Betty can get you up again" and she went back to sucking my dick. When she had me hard again she climbed on me and lowered herself onto my hard cock and began to ride me.

"Like my pussy baby? You can have it as much as you want. It's your reward for being my friend tonight. That's it baby, fuck me. You like slut's baby? I'm a slut. After tonight Marlene will be one too. She'll want to do it again baby. She'll be just like me after my first time. Harry has a big cock and Marlene will want more of it. I know, because I can't get enough of it either. Will you like that baby? Will you like being married to a slut? She won't just look like one anymore, she'll be one, just like me. She'll want lots of cock, just like me. Will you fuck her when you go home? Slide your hard cock into her cum filled pussy? Will you go down on her? Taste the cum in her mouth when you kiss her?

"I lied to you baby. No one put anything in her drink. She's across the hall because she wants to be baby. She's always been a slut at heart. She's always wanted to do what she's doing across the hall, she just needed the right circumstances. She's a slut baby, and she always has been and she has just been waiting to turn it loose. All Harry had to do tonight was to get her out on the back porch alone and take out his big cock for her to see. It's eleven inches baby and as big around as my wrist. Your slut wife took one look at it and went to her knees and kissed it. I know she did baby because I watched her do it. I was Harry's lookout to warn him if any one came along. Someone like the silly husband who didn't know what a slut he was married to. You like knowing she's a slut baby? You like fucking sluts like me and your wife? Ron fucked her too. He's got a ten-inch cock baby and your little whore is now hooked on big cocks. Know why she's fucking all those guys over there? Because Harry and Ron told her she couldn't have their big cocks again unless she did.

"Marlene is a slut for big cocks now baby and she will do whatever Ron and Harry tells her to do from now on. By this time next week she will be fucking their friends, their customers, their suppliers, anyone they want her to just so she can get some more of their big cocks. She'll be real popular with the guys since she looks so slutty. She'll still cook and clean for you baby and she will fuck you as much as you want, but she doesn't belong to you anymore. Harry and Ron own her now. You'll like being married to a slut baby, we are always so hot, wet and ready to fuck."

Her talking was driving me crazy and I grabbed her hips and thrust into her as hard as I could and my cock erupted and sprayed her insides with my cum.

"Ah, that's it baby, fill me up. Fill your new slut up with your cum. I'm going to suck you hard again baby and then you are going to fuck my ass. I love it in my ass baby and you can have it any time you want."

She did get me hard again and I did fuck her in her ass and when I was exhausted and lying there on the bed next to her she said to me:

"I meant it baby. You can fuck me whenever you want. Just call and I'll be waiting."

We got dressed and left the bedroom and I saw that the door to the master bedroom was open and there was no one inside.

"Go and find your brand new slut baby, but don't forget the one you just fucked. I'll be waiting for your call."

The party was still going strong when I got back downstairs and I saw Marlene talking to some woman in the kitchen. She looked the same as she had when we had arrived, but sluttier, if you know what I mean. I stood looking at her knowing that she was now every bit the slut she looked and I wondered if Betty was right. Would she want more cock now? If she did how was I going to handle it? I walked over to her and said:

"There you are. I've been looking all over for you."

She looked up at me and said, "I needed some fresh air and Betty and I went out for a walk."

I looked at her and knew that Betty was right. My wife had become a slut and was planning on being an unfaithful one at that. I had no idea how she planned on hiding it from me, but I had a hunch that with Betty's help I'd know when and where. All I had to do now was figure out how long I wanted to fuck Betty. I knew I would stop getting Betty's pussy when I kicked Marlene's cheating ass out on the street.

End of the 5th Story

Martha's Revenge

"You what?" I said to what my sister had just asked me.

"You heard me," she said.

"I know I heard you, but I just don't believe I heard you right."

"But you did little brother, you did. I'll be over in a little bit to tell you about it."

My sister Martha is three years older than I am, but we couldn't be closer if we were twins. I don't know or even remember how the tone of our relationship started, but it has been a raunchy one for as long as I can remember. When she was in high school she made it a habit to let me see her naked just so she could laugh when she gave me a hard on. Once I hit fifteen it was payback time. I used to barge in on her when she was in the bathtub, haul out my hose and take a pee in front of her and then give it a couple of strokes while she watched and then say, "Sorry Sis, you can't have it. You're family, you know?"

And it got worse. One night I walked into her bedroom to get a couple of my records that she had borrowed and found her using a rubber dick on herself. I unzipped, walked over and stood in front of her, stroked myself until I got hard and then said, "Here! You can look at this one while you use the phony."

She got even with me two weeks later when I was in my bedroom and about to slide my dick into the next door neighbor's daughter. In walked Martha and she said, "Here stud. Don't forget to use these" and she tossed me a package of Trojans. Poor Merrily was so embarrassed that she got up and ran home.

It was all good natured and even enjoyable at times, like when she set me up with one of her girlfriends.

"All she wants, brother mine, is a good, hard, no frills fuck with no attachments."

Well, I did the job, but the no attachments part didn't stick. Janice and I made it for three months before she found someone her own age to do what I'd been doing. Martha and I even went on double dates a couple of times and I fucked my date in the front seat while she took on hers in the back. Another time she fucked her boyfriend on the couch while I stood at the front window keeping an eye out for mom and dad.

It has slacked off a lot since Martha got married, but I can still expect surprises from her. Just last birthday I opened the present she brought me and then had to quickly shut the box so no one else could see what was inside - two dozen condoms, a fake rubber pussy, and a card that said, "Think Safe Sex." So when she called me today with her request I didn't know if she was kidding, setting me up for something, or what.

***

"You heard me right," she said across the kitchen table, "I want you to find me one of your black friends who would be willing to be videotaped fucking me in my ass."

I looked at her like she was crazy; "This is a joke, right?"

"No joke little brother, just plain old revenge."

Martha had caught her husband cheating on her, not just once but several times, and each time he had begged forgiveness and promised never to do it again. The last time, however, he'd gotten caught doing it in the marital bed. Martha intended to punish Bill in the most humiliating way she could think of, by letting a black man fuck her; no, not just fuck her, but fuck her in her ass and tape it so she could show him the video.

Now to understand why this could be considered revenge you would have to know her husband Bill. All in all, a pretty nice guy, easy to get along with (too easy according to Martha), but he did have one major flaw - he was a racist and he had absolutely no use for minorities. In a partial defense of him it should be said that he was born and raised in South Carolina and his prejudice was built into him by family and friends from the day he was old enough to walk. It didn't help that he had never left the state until he was thirty. I did have to agree that if she wanted to get to him she had chosen the most guaranteed way.

But I did have a question, "Why in the ass? Wouldn't just doing it on tape do the job?"

"It might," she said, "But I don't like it anal and I won't let Billy do me there, so letting a black man do it should send him to the moon."

I gave her the most serious look I could muster and said, "And when he goes and gets a gun and comes looking for you, what then?" She smiled and said,

"I'll be out of the house by then and living here with you. You will protect me, won't you?"

I spent another hour trying to talk her out of it, but she had her mind made up and so, with great reluctance, I told her I would help.

***

Martha is 5' 6", 120 lbs, with 36C cup tits and raven black hair that hangs all the way down to her ass. She's had boys sniffing after her since she was thirteen and old enough to know what they were trying to sniff. So getting someone to fuck shouldn't be a problem, right? Wrong!

"What's wrong with her that she has to have you find somebody to do her?" was the most common response that I got and, "Shit man, I don't want to take no chance on getting AIDS. Poopchute fucking is a no no nowadays" was the next most common. My favorite was, "Yeah, right! I'll be in the saddle going for glory when that cracker son of a bitch comes crashing through the door with a shotgun."

By the end of the week I hadn't found anyone (anyone black) willing to fuck the best looking woman in town - totally unbelievable!

Just when I thought that I was fighting a lost cause I got some help from none other than Bill himself. Clarissa Maggus was bent over trying to change a flat tire when Bill came by. He started to slow down and give her a hand, but when Clarissa stood up and Bill saw that she was black he swung back on the road and drove away. The next day Clarissa's brother Roy came to see he and me was pissed, "Does your sister still want to hang horns on that miserable son of a bitch?"

I nodded my head yes and Roy said, "Then I'm your man."

I called Martha and gave her the news and asked her where and when.

"Tomorrow night and can I use your place? I don't want to take a chance on Billy coming home before I'm through."

I was quiet for a moment and then I said, "I hope you don't expect me to be there when you do this."

"You have to be there!" she cried, "I need you to take the video."

I laughed at that one, "I don't think so. For God's sake Martha, you're my sister. I'll grant you that we're close and I've watched you get screwed before, but I can't watch you get screwed by somebody else and take pictures of it. When that gets out, and you know that it will, I'll have the reputation in this town of some kind of sexual pervert."

Martha begged and pleaded and against my better judgement, she finally talked me into it using the argument that she might need me to protect her from Bill. I was not a happy camper, but she was my sister and Bill was going to be outraged when he found out what she'd done. And, as I've mentioned earlier, it wouldn't be the first time I'd watched her get laid.

***

There were times when I hated Martha and this was one of them.

"How do I look?" she asked as she spun around in front of me in only thigh highs and high heels. I looked at her and cursed the fates that made her my sister. Right at that moment I wanted her so bad that I felt actual physical pain, but instead of being able to have her I was going to have to watch as someone else took her. The doorbell rang and I opened the door to find Roy standing there, but he wasn't alone.

"I brought Vernon and George to watch my back just in case that cracker bastard finds out what's going on and comes over. They'll wait outside in the car, but I wanted you to know that they are here."

From behind me I heard Martha say, "They don't have to stay in the car. They can wait in the living room." I turned to look at her and she said, "I know what I'm doing. If they stay in the car they will always wonder if Roy was telling them the truth. In the living room they'll know it's true because they will hear what's happening. Then they will tell all their friends and everybody will start looking at Billy with smirks on their faces. Don't forget little brother, this isn't about getting me laid, it's about humiliating Billy."

I just stood aside and let the three of them walk in and all three developed instant erections as soon as they saw Martha standing there. Martha smiled sweetly and said, "Thanks for helping me out on this Roy. I'll try and make it worth your while."

She took him by the hand and led him to the bedroom and I watched Vernon and George watch her walk away. I couldn't help but laugh, "Hey, I asked both of you and you both turned me down."

I picked up the video camera and followed Martha and Roy down the hall. Martha was undressing Roy when I got there so I moved off to the side and started filming. She got his shirt off and stood on tiptoe to kiss him while she undid his belt and pulled down his zipper. The pants fell to the floor and Roy kicked off his loafers and stepped out of the pants while Martha, still on tiptoe and kissing him, slid her hand into his shorts and started playing with his cock. Martha broke the kiss and went to her knees and pulled down his briefs.

As his erect cock leapt free she leaned forward and captured it with her mouth and held it while she worked his shorts and then his socks off of him. Her hands went to Roy's hips and she held him while sucking his cock and as I watched that black pole disappear into that white face my cock twitched and I knew that I was going to keep a copy of the tape for myself. For the next couple of minutes Martha did not suck Roy's cock, she made love to it, several times looking over at the camera and winking. I thought about what an ignorant bastard Bill was to have fucked up and thrown Martha away.

Martha got up and led Roy to the bed and she lay down and spread her legs, "Fuck me in my pussy first baby. I need to warm up a little before you take my ass."

I moved to the side of the bed and zoomed in on that black cock sliding into Martha's pussy and I knew that Bill would be grinding his teeth when he saw it. I pulled back to wide angle and then moved around the bed catching different angles as Roy fucked Martha. The sound track alone would drive Bill nuts, "That's it baby, push that black cock into me. Oh god that feels good. Fuck me baby, fuck me hard. Oh god, oh god, oh god, harder baby, harder. Oh god, oh god, I'm cumming, I'm cumming. Hold me baby, hold me. Come on baby, give it to me, give it to me hard. That's it baby, cum for me, cum for me baby, cum for me."

I didn't exactly know how Bill was going to react, but it was killing me. Then came the part that would send Bill over the edge; Roy said "I'm gonna cum, gonna cum" and Martha said, "In me baby, in me, shoot it deep in me."

I saw movement out of the corner of my eye and turned to see George and Vernon standing just inside the bedroom door. They both had their dicks out and were jacking off while watching the action on the bed. Back on the bed Roy was just getting off of Martha and she took one look at his limp dick and asked, "How fast can you get it back up?"

Roy gave a little chuckle and said, "With your magic mouth? Maybe three or four minutes."

Martha smiled and said, "Bring it here baby, let Martha help."

As Roy was changing positions Martha noticed the other two in the room and she looked at me. I didn't know what to say so I just shrugged. Martha turned her attention back to Roy and started sucking his cock. Two minutes into the blow job she stopped and looked over at George and Vernon. She started to turn her attention back to Roy and then stopped. She got off the bed and had Roy move over to the side of the bed and then stood next to the bed and she went back to sucking his cock. Thirty seconds later she stopped, turned to George and Vern and said, "Doesn't my standing here, bent over at the waist with my legs spread mean anything to you guys?"

Both guys dropped their pants and rushed over to Martha. George got there first and he slid right into Martha with no trouble. Vern being the slow one had to settle for standing off to the side so Martha could give him a hand job. Martha turned to me, "Make sure you get all of this little brother, don't miss a thing."

I was not only getting it, but it was getting to me. Roy's cock grew as Martha worked on it and finally Roy said, "It's ready for you honey," and George said, "Hold on, hold on, I'm almost there, I'm going to cum, I'm cumming baby, I'm cumming" and Martha pushed back at him and moaned, "Give it to me baby, give it to me. Shoot it in me baby, cum in me, cum in me."

I zoomed in on her face as she licked the head of Roy's cock and then pulled back to get a shot of the cum running down her leg as George pulled out of her and she sucked the head of Roy's dick. Then I pulled back a little further and got a group shot of Martha jacking off Vern, while George was pulling out of her and she still had her mouth on Roy. Martha let go of Vern and he hurried behind her and slid his dick into dripping mess that was her pussy. I had moved around to where I could get a close up of Martha's face as Vern slid his cock into her and the look on her face was pure lust and as Vern entered her, she moaned, "Oh yes, oh god yes. Fuck me baby, slide that black piece of meat in me and fuck me hard."

I moved back off to the side and got a wide-angle shot of Martha bent forward with her elbows resting on the bed as Vern plowed her from behind. Vern was the one who was really going to upset Bill. Both Roy and George were light brown, but Vern was coal black and his blackness and Martha's whiteness were startling when seen together. Vern took about five minutes before he said he was going to cum and when he said he was ready Martha looked right into the camera and cried, "In me, I want it in me, fill me up baby, fill me up."

Again, I zoomed in on Martha's pussy when that black cock slowly withdrew and shot the small stream of cum that followed it out and ran down the inside of her leg. I walked over to her and bent down to whisper in her ear, "You are going to have to do without a cameraman for a little bit. I need to get rid of this major problem that watching you has caused."

She gave me a look that I'd never seen from her before and said, "Oh baby, I'm sorry. I didn't even think of that" and then there was a moment's hesitation and she said "I'll take care of you little brother" and she reached for my belt buckle.

I backed away, "No! I would love it, but not with these guys here. It won't hurt your reputation when it gets out what you are doing with these guys and why. It just means that more guys will come sniffing around. If word got out that you did me, we would both have to leave town."

"Honey," George said, "You can come and live with me if you need a place to stay. I'll let you do that all day and all night."

Martha giggled and said, "Thank you baby. You've got a nice cock. I just might take you up on that."

Roy, who had been holding still, said "Brace yourself honey. It will hurt for a minute or so and then it will get better" and with that he started making short strokes and working his cock into her butthole. I didn't want her facial expressions while she was showing pain so I zoomed in on Roy's cock as it moved back and forth in Martha's ass. Roy went slow and it took him almost three minutes to get his entire cock all the way in. He kept making short strokes until Martha's moaning started changing to "oh, oh, oh" and then to "Oh yes, oh yes, oh yes" and finally to "Oh god, oh god, oh god yes, fuck me, fuck me, fuck me."

I pulled back to wide angle and filmed Roy as his strokes became longer, but he still kept it slow and easy until Martha cried out, "Fuck me god damn it, fuck my ass, fuck me hard."

Roy started pounding at her ass and Martha was going, "So good, so good, oh god fuck me, please don't stop fucking me" and then her voice was choked off and I looked to see that Vern had climbed onto the bed and he had his dick in Martha's mouth.

After that it got repetitious. All three guys fucked Martha in the butt, she sucked some more cock, got fucked in the pussy a couple of more times and I was on my fifth thirty minute tape when she did the ultimate - she took all three of them at once - one in her mouth, one in her ass and one in her pussy. It was mind blowing to see her being bounced around and trying to handle all that cock. It was two in the morning when the three guys left a very fucked out Martha lying on my bed. They all told her that they would love to do it again and would be available if she ever got the urge.

"I won't rule it out," she said, "I kind of liked it."

When they were gone she said, "You do know I'm your new roommate, right? I can't go home after this so you are stuck with me until I can find a place of my own."

I said, "I don't mind, as long as you don't do any more of these things and make me film them."

She chuckled and said, "That was my first time with more than one guy and I really think I could learn to like it."

Well, she did, but that's another story. The rest of this story is that I transferred the five thirty minute tapes to a six hour VHS tape and Martha Fed-Exed it to Bill along with a short note that said, "Just something for you to watch when you aren't fucking Annie, Beatrice, Debbie, Angela, your secretary or that big titted barmaid down at Andy's."

His response wasn't anywhere near what Martha expected, but that's also for another story. As for the curious among you, no, I did not fuck my sister after the guys left and we were alone, but the attraction is there and who knows, maybe another story there too.

***

Martha Fed-Exed Bill the tape on Thursday morning and Saturday at noon he was beating on my front door. When I opened the door he said, "Is she here?"

I nodded a yes and he said, "I need to talk to her."

I told him that I didn't think she wanted to see him, but I'd go ask and I closed the door on him. I walked back to the kitchen where Martha was making us lunch and said, "Guess who is here and wants to talk to you?" She looked up from the sink at me and I said, "Yes indeedy, it is your very own ex-true love."

She shook her head no, "I don't have anything to say to the man - the tape said it all."

I went back to the door and told Bill what she'd said.

"Come on man, you have to help me here. I know I've given her reason to be pissed, but I have to talk to her. Keep the screen door locked and stand next to her if you feel the need, but I have to talk to her."

Once again I closed the door on him and went back to the kitchen. "He's still here and he still wants to talk. I think you should do it and get it out of the way. He'll just hang around until you do."

Martha said, "I don't really want to, but if it will get rid of him I guess I'd better. But I want you in the next room in case I holler."

I left the two of them talking through the screen door and I went into the living room to give them some privacy. About five minutes later Martha stuck her head in the living room and told me that she was letting him in and they were going into the kitchen to talk. Half an hour later I heard him leave and I went out to the kitchen. Martha was sitting at the kitchen table and she had a strange look on her face, "You won't believe this little brother, but that tape turned him on. He wants to know if he can be there if I ever do it again."

I looked at her and I'm sure that she could see the skepticism on my face because she said, "I know, I know, it doesn't sound at all like Billy, but he says that tape is the most erotic thing he has ever seen and he has watched it over and over ever since he got it. He didn't beg me for forgiveness or to come back to him or anything like that. He just wants to be there if I do it again." Then she gave me a long look and said, "I loved doing what I did, but I only intended to do it once, and only then to get back at Billy. But I have to tell you that I'm tempted to do it again just so I can watch his face." Again she read my face, "You don't think it's a good idea, do you?"

I just nodded my head no.

"Why not?" she asked.

"Can a dog change his spots? Do you think that someone with his history of racial hatred is going to do a one-eighty that quickly?"

She grinned at me and said, "Little brother, when it comes to their dicks I've seen some pretty damn quick changes in guys."

"Yeah," I said, "But what if what he really wants is to get you and the guys together in one room he can haul out a gun and do you all at the same time?"

She gave me an amused look, "Not my Billy little brother, not my Billy."

I didn't say anything for a bit and then I asked, "So, are you going to do it?"

It was her turn to be silent and then she said, "I don't know. I'll have to think on it."

I had a bad night, but then all of my nights had been bad since Martha's gangbang and her moving in with me. All I had to do was remember that night and I'd get a hard dick, and having a hard dick with Martha just down the hall was pure agony. I knew that if I went to her room she wouldn't chase me away, just as I knew that she knew that I wouldn't run her off if she came to me. Again and again I cursed the fates that made us brother and sister. The morning got off to a very bad start with Martha telling me over breakfast that she had decided to call Roy, Vernon and George and see if they would be willing to do it again with Bill in the room. If they said no that would be the end of it, but if they said yes she wanted me to be there in the role of peacekeeper. She saw the look on my face and said, "Please baby, please?"

What the hell could I say except yes. It was a good thing it was Sunday because I wouldn't have gotten a damn thing done if I'd had to go to work. About noon Martha asked me if I would call Roy and I blew up on her, "No fucking way. I might have to suffer through being there, but I am not going to be your fucking pimp! You want to do this, you call him!" and I stomped out of the room.

I went outside and changed the oil in my car and then rotated the tires and when I came back in she said, "Is Tuesday okay with you?"

"No day is going to be good for me, but the sooner we get it over with the better."

The rest of the day didn't get any better for me; Martha, Roy and the rest of the guys kept intruding on my thoughts so I decided that just mind numbing physical labor was what I needed. A cleaning out of the basement and then the garage was long overdue so I spent the rest of the day hauling boxes up out of the basement and stacking them in the garage. I'd use Monday to sort through them before putting them out for trash - anything to keep my mind off Martha.

Monday was another bad day for me. I got out of bed and headed for the bathroom. Just as I got there, the door opened and Martha came out. She was naked except for a towel wrapped around her head and the sight of her high pointed breasts gave me an instant hard on. Martha noticed it and said, "Is that for me little brother?" She chuckled, "If you want to give it to me I'll be more than happy to take it."

"God damned tease!" I snarled as I went into the bathroom and slammed the door. I could hear her laugh echo down the hallway as she went to her room. That set the tone for the rest of the day and the entire time I was at work, images of Martha kept intruding on my mind; Martha coming out of the bathroom, Martha and Roy, Martha and all three of the guys in her. I finally reached the point where I couldn't take it anymore and I told the boss I wasn't feeling well and I took the rest of the day off and went home.

I still needed to occupy my mind and my time so when I got home I started sorting through all the stuff I'd brought out of the basement. The first box was full of papers and legal stuff that the lawyer had given me when mom and dad had died. I really didn't need any more emotional baggage on that particular day so I set it aside for later. As I dug through the rest of the stuff I found pretty much what I expected; stuff that had been moved from house to house over the years and had never been used. In the end, out of seventeen boxes that I'd hauled out of the basement three went to Goodwill, one went back to the basement and the rest went out to the curb for trash pick-up. Mom and dad's personal papers stayed in the garage for another day.

Martha came home from work and fixed us dinner, but it was a pretty silent meal. Finally Martha said, "I'm sorry little brother. I know I shouldn't tease you, but sometimes I just can't help it. It's just that I want you so bad and I know we can't and it gets so damn frustrating. I'll find a place soon - I promise - and then we won't be around each other to tempt fate."

I said, "It would help one hell of a lot if I didn't have to be around you while you're fucking over Bill."

She gave me a sad smile and said, "I'm sorry baby, I know I'm asking a lot of you, but this time you don't have to film it. Just be in the next room in case I have to call for help."

Tuesday at work was no better than Monday had been, if anything it was worse because I knew what would be happening that night. I couldn't afford to miss any more time off work so I just had to suffer through the day. At dinner that evening Martha told me that she had changed her mind and that she did want me to tape the evening's festivities, "If Billy gives me any shit I'll mail it to his family and let them see him standing there watching black men fucking me."

I was not a happy camper.

I called Roy about five o'clock just out of curiosity and asked him why he had agreed to do it knowing that Bill was going to be there.

"Simple," he told me, "I just want to rub that redneck bastard's nose in it. I want him to hear his wife begging me to fuck her hard. Do me a favor and ask her if, when I get ready to cum, she'll holler "in me baby, as deep in me as you can."

I shook my head, "Sorry, you have to understand how weird this is for me in the first place. I can't carry messages like that."

Bill was the first one to arrive and I took advantage of the fact that we were alone to ask him why he was doing it.

"I don't honestly know. I saw that tape and I knew as soon as I saw it what she was trying to do, and I guess I deserved it, but the tape got to me on some level and it turned me on like nothing ever had before. I've watched it over two dozen times since I got it and when I'm not watching it I'm thinking about it. I guess that makes me pretty fucked up, huh?"

I didn't figure I could answer that one, not given the way the tape affected me. He went on, "Maybe what I'm really hoping for is that seeing it in person will disgust me enough that I'll get up and leave and never look back. On the other hand maybe what I want more that anything is to take Martha home and treat her the way I always was supposed to, so she'll never have to do anything like this again. I honestly don't know."

Bill was sitting in the easy chair in the living room when Martha came in to the living room in nothing but high heels, nylons and a garter belt. She did a slow turn and said, "How do I look guys?"

Bill looked at her and I could see the hunger on his face, but all he said was, "You look very nice Martha."

She turned toward me, but I was saved from having to say

anything by the doorbell. It was Roy and George and while I was holding the door open for them, Vernon hurried up the walk. I went and got the video camera and when I came back Martha had everyone arranged. Bill was still in the easy chair and the three guys were sitting next to each other on the couch naked from the waist down. Martha glanced over at Bill to see how he was taking it and then she knelt in front of the three black men.

For the next ten minutes she went from one end of the couch to the other and then back to sucking one cock after the other while I filmed the action. I kept cutting away from the couch to catch the look on Bill's face. He was so engrossed in what was happening in front of him that I don't believe he even noticed me taking pictures. Finally Martha stood up and led the boys into the bedroom. Martha had set a chair right next to the bed and she pointed at it when Bill came into the room, "Billy, you sit down right there and you behave yourself, you hear?"

The next two hours were basically a repeat of the first night with the only change being Martha's comments to Bill as the action progressed. It was obvious to me that, like Roy, her intent was to rub Bill's nose in it. She began by having Roy lie down on the bed and then she bent over and took his cock in her mouth. She licked him a few times and then turned to Vernon and George and said, "Okay, who is going to be first?" George moved up behind her and Martha looked at Bill and said, "Watch him slide that nice black cock in me while I suck Roy's hard black dick."

I saw the smile on Roy's face as he looked Bill right in the eye as Martha's lips closed around him. I filmed George ramming his cock in Martha while her head bobbed up and down on Roy and then I moved to a close up of Bill's face. Any doubt I might have had over his real reason for being there that night vanished when I saw the expression on his face. Roy and Martha might have thought they were rubbing his nose in it, but Bill was turned on big time. I pulled back to a wide-angle shot and it showed Bill staring at what was happening on the bed while squeezing the lump in his trousers; he was enjoying the hell out of this!

It took almost five minutes and then George announced that he was going to cum and Martha took her mouth off of him long enough to say, "Fill me up baby. Shoot it down my throat" and the she went back to sucking Roy. In less than a minute cum was leaking out of the corners of Martha's mouth and running down her chin. She released Roy's cock long enough to look over at Bill and slowly lick her chin. It was at that moment, looking into Bill's face while she licked Roy's cum off of her chin, that she realized that what she was doing was not punishing Bill at all and that in fact, the more wanton she got with her black lovers, the more Bill would like it.

She told Vernon that she wanted him in her ass and then she turned so she could look directly into Bill's eyes as Vernon fed his cock into her tight anal orifice. She talked him all the way through it, "That's it baby, easy, go slow baby, go easy on me. Aw god does that feel good. Slide that big black sausage into my tight little asshole. Oh Jesus, but I do like black cock in my ass. That's it baby, fuck me now, fuck my ass." She kept that up until Vernon told her was going to cum. "Do it baby, do it. Fill my ass with your cum," she moaned.

After Vernon, George fucked her in her ass and then so did Roy. After Roy had fired his load in her butt she said, "My poor pussy is feeling neglected guys. Won't someone please slide a hard black cock into my wet pussy?"

All three guys fucked her and then she told them to relax. "Next I want all three of you at once so I want you all rested, hard and ready to go at the same time."

I had been shooting tape of all this and I kept going back to Bill's face. He was showing great restraint, but I could tell that more than anything he wanted to be part of the action. I could hardly blame him because I had the same feelings. When the three guys took Martha at the same time, ass, pussy and mouth, Bill couldn't hold back any longer. He opened his pants, took out his cock and began beating off. At that point I felt guilty about taping his reactions to what Martha was doing on the bed and I turned the camera off.

Martha was still taunting him. As she serviced her three black lovers she kept bombarding Bill with "Oh god yes, you guys feel so good. I love your beautiful black cocks in me. That's it, fuck me boys, fuck me good. Watch them Billy, watch them stuff me full of hard black meat. Watch them fuck your wife with their hard black cocks. Does it turn you on Billy? Does it make your dick hard to see your whore wife with all these black cocks in her?"

Bill was so intent on watching that when he got himself off, he blew his load all over the front of his pants. I saw Roy smirk when it happened and I wondered again why Bill was willing to subject himself to all this abuse. For the next hour, the three men took turns using Martha's ass, mouth and pussy. Finally Martha said, "Why don't you boys run along now. I think me and my hubby need to talk."

Roy, Vernon and George got dressed and headed for the door, but just before they got there Martha said, "Thursday night? Same time?"

The guys all grinned and said that they would be there. When they were gone Martha said to Bill, "Well? Did it turn you on as much as you thought?"

Bill croaked out a hoarse "yes." "Do you want to fuck your whore wife?" Again the croaked yes. "You mean that you are willing to stick your lily white cock into the accumulated cum of three black men?" Bill stood up and undressed, but as he approached the bed, Martha laughed at him, "Not so fast Billy. You have to earn the right to fuck this slut for black cock. Are you willing to pay the price?"

Bill said in a voice that cracked just a little, "Whatever I have to do, I'll do it."

Martha looked surprised, she hadn't expected this, but then she gave him an evil grin, "Eat my pussy Billy. Get down there and lick up all that black cum and then I'll let you fuck me."

At that moment I didn't like my sister very much and I left the room, but I guess Bill did what she wanted him to do because later I heard her cry out, "That's it baby, fuck me, fuck me hard."

The next morning I awoke to a strange feeling. I had dreamt that I was fucking Martha and when I woke up my dick was hard and it did feel like it was being used. I looked down and saw Martha with her hand on my cock and looking up at me. "Good" she said, "I wanted you awake for this" and she took my cock in her mouth. I wanted to push her away, to say that this was wrong and that we couldn't do it, but I didn't. I just lay there and enjoyed it. It only took her two or three minutes to get me off and when I came it seemed to me like I emptied buckets full into her mouth. She gulped and gulped and managed to swallow it all and when my cock was finally soft she removed her mouth from it and licked it clean.

She crawled up next to me and put her arms around me and said, "I owed you that little brother for all I've put you through lately. And as far as I'm concerned it's not wrong. The laws on incest are there to prevent close family members from making babies and I can't get pregnant from giving you a blow job."

Regardless of what Martha said I still didn't feel right about what happened, but I do have to admit that at work that day I felt better than I had in a long time. Martha told me over breakfast that Bill had asked her to come home with him, but she had said no, at least not for the time being. He had begged and had even said that she could have Roy, Vernon and George over anytime she wanted. In fact, he'd even said she could have as many guys as she wanted from now on if she would just come back to him and let him be there to watch.

"I don't know little brother, I need to think on it a little more. I have to admit that I'm beginning to love having more than one man at a time, but I'm not sure that I want to do it as often as Billy sounds like he wants me to."

That left a question and so I asked it, "Do you love him? Love him enough to go back to him? And what about the running around he did, can you forget that?"

She was quiet for a while and then said, "Yeah, I love him. He's an asshole sometimes, but I love him. As far as the running around goes, maybe Roy, the boys and me can keep him closer to home. And if he does wander off I'll have the guys to keep me from getting lonely, or some guys anyway. Billy has done that much for me. He's shown me that variety is indeed the spice of life."

That night when I got home, I attacked the last of the boxes in the garage. It was the personal papers of mom and dad and most of it had no meaning or value now that they were gone; things like their marriage license, a deed of trust on their house that Martha and I had inherited, some loan papers stamped "Paid in Full" and some photographs. There was a brown envelope at the bottom of the box and I opened it. It was a three-page document and I read it, and then read it again and then again for a third time as what it meant finally sunk in.

I fixed dinner that night and Martha and I had a bottle of Merlot with the meal. We talked some about what the future had in store for her if she continued to have black lovers and if she got back together with Bill. We cleared the table and did the dishes and then took another bottle of wine and went into the living room and sat down on the couch.

"You have another problem that's going to have to be solved soon."

"What?" she said.

"Me. I've been at both your sessions with the guys and it has me walking around with a permanent hard on because of it."

She giggled and said, "Let me see" and she came over and sat down in my lap and wiggled her butt. "Ooh, it is hard. Should I do something about it?" and then she kissed me.

It was not a sisterly kiss and she was surprised when I returned it with the same intensity a man would show his wife or his lover. When we broke the kiss I told her that yes indeed she should do something about my hard on, "But that isn't the problem that needs to be solved."

"Oh?" she asked, "Just what is this big problem then?"

I fished a folded piece of paper out of my shirt pocket and handed it to her. "We have to decide which side of the bed you are going to sleep on."

She read the paper and then looked up at me, "Race you to the bedroom!" she said as my adoption papers fell to the floor.

It was almost five months before Martha went back home to Bill and we spent every night of those five months in my bed making up for lost time. During that period Martha also saw Roy, Vernon, George and one or two of their friends once a week or so with Bill watching and then eating her out and fucking her. He would leave and she would jump in bed with me and we would spend the rest of the night fucking.

Most everybody still thinks Martha and I are blood relations and we haven't done anything to correct that impression because it is easier for our neighbors to accept that a brother and sister are sharing a house. Especially since it is well known that she is estranged from her husband.

We did let Bill, Roy and the rest of the boys know so that they wouldn't be scandalized when I joined in the weekly gangbang. Bill has gone from watching to participating and, surprising the hell out of me and Martha, has become good friends with Roy, George and Vernon. He has even had their families over to his house for a barbecue.

It will be interesting to see how long his friendship with Roy lasts. Roy is pretty close to his sister Clarissa's husband and Bill has been fucking Clarissa for about a month now. How do I know? He brings her over to my place. Martha's reaction to his fucking other women? She thinks it's kinky especially when she is fucking me on the bed next to Bill and Clarissa, and even kinkier when we swap partners. Clarissa knows about Martha, Roy, Vernon and George and she has been after Bill to get her a "couple more white guys" so she can experience what it's like and Bill wants to do it - where else? - at my place. This prompted Martha to tell Bill to get a bunch more guys because she plans to be there also. I have no idea where this is going or what the end might be like, but for now life is good and I'm loving it.

End of the 6th Story

Sticking It To Peggy

I stood there at the window and watched as the car backed down the drive, turned right and then disappeared down the street. I wondered why I wasn't more upset. I'd just seen ten years of my life drive away. Shouldn't I have felt something? Shouldn't there have been something other than a shrug of the shoulders and an, "Oh well; I guess I should go and take care of that dripping faucet?" As I turned and headed for the kitchen, I ran the events of the last half hour back through my mind.

I'd come home from work to find my wife Peggy sitting at the kitchen table with a full glass of wine sitting in front of her. I knew something was up as soon as I saw her sitting there. First - she was home before me and she never got home from work until a half hour to an hour after I did. Secondly - the understanding we had was the first one home would start dinner and there was nothing on the stove. Lastly - there was the glass of wine. Peg rarely drank. I was no sooner in the room than she asked me to sit down and told me she had something to say. I grabbed a beer out of the fridge, sat down across from her and she said:

"Rob, I know you know this. There has been something out of sync between us for the last six months or so. I have no idea why we seem to be moving away from each other. I don't know if it is something to do with me or something to do with you, but something is wrong. I've tried to talk with you about it, but all I get from you is that we are just going through a rough spot and it will get better. I've decided that we need to separate. I'm not talking divorce, just a separation for a while.

"I think I need some space Rob. I need to get away, look at my life and see if I can figure out where the disconnection between us is coming from. You can use the time we are apart to look at the same thing from your angle."

"Oh come on Peg; it isn't that bad. Sure we are having some problems - what marriage doesn't - but two people can't work out problems if they are away from each other and not talking."

"Talking isn't going to help Rob. You only see one problem with our marriage. As far as you are concerned the only problem we have is that we aren't making love. Your solution to the problem is for me to get naked and let you have your way with me. As far as I'm concerned there is a lot more wrong. We don't make love anymore because I don't want to. We don't snuggle or cuddle anymore because I don't want you touching me and I don't know why I don't want you to touch me. I still love you. I love you as much as I did on the day we were married, but something is wrong and I don't know what it is. I need some space Rob; I need some time alone so I can figure things out."

"So you want to pitch ten years of marriage out the window."

"No Rob; I just think we need to spend some time apart. I've already packed my stuff in my car. I'm going to stay with my sister until I can find me a place. I'll call you once a week to keep in touch."

She stood up and said, "I have to go. I told Mary that I'd be there by seven." She turned and walked away without even offering to kiss me goodbye and that in itself told me where I stood.

***

It didn't take long for the word to get around that Peggy and I had separated. Most of our friends were sympathetic and went out of their way to try and cheer me up. Peggy called me once a week and asked me how I was and I would say I was managing and then I'd ask her how she was and she would say that she was okay. Then I would ask her if she were ready to come home yet and she would tell me not yet.

Peg had been gone for six weeks when I started hearing things; disturbing things. Things like she had a live-in boyfriend. I didn't want to believe that. I wanted to believe that things were like she said they were; that she just wanted some time alone to get her head straight and then she would be coming home. I kept hearing things so I decided to check out the rumors. I'd find out where Peg was staying, do a little snooping and put the rumors to rest. But no one could tell me where she was staying, either couldn't or wouldn't, and I began to think that something about the situation stunk to high heaven.

I was having dinner with my friend Tom and his wife Tanya and I voiced my concerns and let slip that I was going to hire a private detective to find Peg and either confirm the rumors or disprove them.

I saw Tom look at Tanya and I saw her give him a little nod. "Save your money Rob," Tom said, "The rumors are true. Most of the people who know you, know what is going on, but they like you too much to tell you."

"Tell me what?"

"That Peggy left you to live with Adam White."

"Adam White? Who the hell is Adam White? I've never heard of him."

"He works with Peggy."

"And she just up and left me to go and live with him? That doesn't make sense. If she was going to do that why didn't she just divorce me? What's with the separation bullshit?"

"You know Peg, Rob. She plans, makes fall back plans and then makes plans if the fall back plan doesn't work. She has been seeing White for almost a year and I'm guessing that she did this separation thing so she could come home if living with White wasn't as good as having an affair with him."

"And everyone knows this, but no one would tell me? Gee, gosh oh golly, what a great bunch of friends I have."

I stood up and threw my napkin down in the center of the table and said, "Thanks bunches. I'll see myself out" and I left their house. On the drive home I thought about what I had just learned. No sex with Peg for over a year because she didn't want to make love with me. No snuggling for over a year because she didn't want me touching her and all the time she was hanging horns on me. Like a fool, I sat at home like a good little boy and behaved myself while I waited for the unfaithful whore to come home. And all my friends - my wonderful friends - knew all about it and they just let me sit there, stare at the walls and wait. Well, the waiting was over.

***

The next morning I made an appointment with the Corliss Investigative Agency and gave them a retainer. I told them where Peg and this White guy worked and told them I wanted all the dirt they could get me on the two and then I went home and started making a list of everything that I needed to do to sever my relationship with Peg. I'd wait until I had the report from the detective agency, but when I got it I would have my list and I would be ready.

Once the list was made I sat back and thought about something else I needed to do. I hadn't been laid in almost sixteen months what with Peg denying me for a year and then the separation. I'd been a completely faithful husband, but now that I knew what Peg was doing I damned sure wasn't going to remain celibate any longer. I sat at the kitchen table sipping a beer and making plans to end my long dry spell when I remembered what Tom had said about Peg.

She planned everything!

After living with her as long as I had, I knew that was true. To me that meant that she had plans for what to do if I found out about what she was doing; plans based on how she thought I would respond to finding out and the biggest plan of all - how to stick it up my ass if she decided that living with White was what she really wanted to do. I could see her having me watched so that if I went out and dipped my wick she would be able to use it against me in a divorce.

All of a sudden the list I had made was worthless because she might have planned for my reacting that way. It was back to the drawing board and a new list took shape and as it took shape I saw that a lot of what I wanted to do would have to be done right away and not left until the last minute. And there were some things that I could do that would stick it up Peg's ass and make her bleed. I smiled at the thought and wondered if she had a plan for when something like that happened to her.

The next morning I went to my bank to deposit my paycheck and while I was there I checked on the safe deposit box that Peg and I had there. I saw from the sign in log that Peg seemed to check the box at least once a week and when I saw that, I knew she was keeping track of me and that at the first sign that I was onto her, she would pounce. I thought about that for a minute and then I took the five certificates of deposit from their plastic envelopes and went upstairs and used the bank's copy machine to copy all five and then I went and put the copies back in their envelopes and put them back in the box. Unless Peg took the CDs out of the envelopes to check them, she would never know about the switch.

Then, since I knew that Peg was checking up on me, I took my passport from the box and casually mentioned to the woman from the bank as she put the box back in its slot, that I was going down to Mexico on a fishing trip. I left the bank with the five CDs in my pocket. I normally was in the bank twice a week on the average and each visit I would cash in one CD, pay the early withdrawal penalty, and then hide the cash away when I got home.

I wasn't a believer in credit cards as I thought you could get in trouble too easily with them so the only ones I had in my name were an American Express, on which the full balance had to be paid when you got the bill, several gasoline company credit cards and one Visa card with a low limit that was in my name only. Peg on the other hand had a good half dozen credit cards in just her name and some of them had high limits. I knew what the limits were because I paid the bills every month and I made a list of the remaining account balances and set it aside. I would make sure that I paid the minimum payment on those cards to keep them in good standing.

I sat down and made a list of all the things that I would like to have and then I went online and over the course of the next couple of weeks I went on a spending binge using Peg's credit cards. When I bailed she would be saddled with the credit card debt and I intended to see that it was considerable. I updated my computer and got a new Dell with all the bells and whistles. I bought a Remington 700 on E-Bay and a whole bunch of other stuff like a digital camera and a state of the art cell phone that did everything but cook my dinner.

The house was Peg's. It had been left to her by her parents so I would have no claim on it, but we had used it as collateral for an open line of credit when we put in the swimming pool and hot tub and both of our signatures were on the account. We had paid off what we had borrowed, but the line of credit was still open. If I timed it right I could draw on that line before she knew what I was doing. I had wondered why when she decided that we needed a trial separation, she packed up and left me in her house instead of asking me to leave. Now I knew. If I was still in the house I would obviously be expecting her to come back. I would obviously see this separation as something that wasn't going to last.

Next, I closed out my 401(k) at work, paid the penalty and the squirreled away the cash. Then I sat back and waited on the private detective's report.

***

The one thing I couldn't figure out how to do was get my ashes hauled. I couldn't take the chance that Peg had someone watching me to see if I did go looking. I decided what I would have to do was leave town on the weekends to go on 'fishing trips.' She knew that I loved to fish and that I went quite often and she knew from the catches I brought home that I did actually go fishing so I doubted that she would pay a private detective to follow me. No need for her to get too carried away, right? After all, wasn't I stupid? Hadn't she been pulling the wool over my eyes for over a year?

It was a Friday and I was just getting ready to leave work when I got a phone call from Tanya asking me to stop by their house on the way home. I tried to beg off, but she told me that it was important, so even though I really didn't want to go there I said I would. When I got there, she let me in and led me into the living room where I found Tom sitting in an easy chair. He got up and offered me his hand and I shook it and then he told me to sit down and get comfortable while he got me a beer.

"Tanya needs to talk with you, Rob and you need to know that I'm 100% on board with what she is going to say."

He left the room and headed for the kitchen while I gave Tanya a questioning look and she said:

"In a minute Rob; you are going to need some beer in you for this."

Tom came back and handed me a Bud and said, "I've got some errands to run and I probably won't be back before midnight. Catch you later" and he headed for the front door and I heard it open and then close behind him. The door closing was Tanya's signal to start talking.

"Rob, you hurt us when you stormed out of here the night you were here for dinner."

I started to say something, but she held up her hand and said, "Let me finish. You were justified, but it still hurt. In our defense all I can say is that we like you a lot and we didn't want to be the ones to hurt you. It gets a little complicated in that we are friends with Peg also and we were hoping she would get her head on straight and go home to you where she belongs. We know you love her, or at least you did love her, but we didn't know if it was enough for you to forgive her so we kept quiet. If you got back together and you didn't know you could have gotten on with your lives without having to worry about forgiving and forgetting. That's it; that's our apology, but that is only part of why Tom and I wanted you to stop by.

"We know you Rob and we know what kind of a guy you are. You would no more cheat on your wife than you would rob a bank. How long has it been since you last had sex?"

The question caught me totally off guard. For the first time I noticed how Tanya was dressed. Low cut blouse that showed off her ample cleavage, short skirt and high heels that show-cased her marvelous legs and friend or no friend I couldn't help but get a hard on. Then I remembered Tom's "I'm a 100% on board" comment and I had an idea where things were going. In a subdued voice I told her that it had been a year and a half.

She leaned toward me and I got a look down inside her blouse as she huskily said:

"I'd like to change that Rob."

"Tom's my friend Tanya; I can't do that to him."

I started to get up, but she grabbed my arm and pulled me back down. "Tom's okay with this Rob, that's why he left, to give us some time alone. This isn't a pity fuck or a mercy fuck Rob. Tom and I have talked this over for months now. You have something we want so hopefully I can help you and you can help us."

"I don't understand what you are saying."

"To be blunt about it Rob, Tom is sterile and we want a child. We want you to give me one."

I was stunned! I sat there and stared at her speechless. When I finally did find my voice I said:

"You just said that you knew I wouldn't cheat on Peg."

"Yes," she said as she laid a hand on the lump in my trousers, "but that was before you knew what Peg was doing. Now that you know you are released from your vows to her."

"Why me?"

"We want it to be someone we know and not some anonymous sperm donor. We are also going to want you to be part of the child's life. You will be the godfather and will always be around as Uncle Rob."

"This doesn't make any sense Tanya."

"Of course it does. What if something happens to Tom and me? Who better to take care of the child than Uncle Rob? On the bad side, God forbid what if the child needed a liver transplant or something like that. Could we find the anonymous sperm donor? And even if we did, would he help? If we got on a waiting list how long would we have to wait to find a donor who would be a match? No Rob, we've thought it through; we want you to be a part of our family. On the other side of the coin, are you going to tell me that you don't find me sexy?"

She squeezed the hard lump in my trousers and said, "This says you do" and then she dropped to her knees in front of me and pulled my zipper down. "There are benefits to being the father of my child Rob. We will have to make love many, many times to make sure that I get pregnant. I won't limit you to just the days I'm most fertile. In fact, I won't even tell you when they are. It could take weeks Rob, weeks and weeks, and you have been without for how long? We will help each other Rob," she said as her lips closed around my cock.

It had been a long time for me and I knew that I wasn't going to last long. I told Tanya and tried to pull out of her mouth, but she grabbed my hips, held tight and sucked harder. "I'm going to cum," I groaned and she locked her lips tight around me and that little bit of additional pressure caused me to explode into her mouth and she kept her mouth tight on me and swallowed everything that came out of my cock. When it started to soften she licked it clean and said:

"Now we can go into the bedroom and do some serious baby making."

All my reservations about what was happening had disappeared about the time my cum shot out of the end of my cock so I got up and followed her into her bedroom. We watched each other undress and then Tanya got on the bed and spread her legs wide.

"From what I've read, the hotter the sex the more receptive the womb is to the invasion of sperm. No loving and tender shit Rob; treat me like a slut, a fuck toy Rob, your fuck toy. Use me, make my blood rush, make me scream and beg and fuck my brains out."

She reached down and pulled the lips of her pussy apart, looked up at me and moaned:

"Put it in Rob; slam your cock into me and breed me."

I climbed on the bed, picked her legs up and put them on my shoulders and then pushed my hard cock into her hot pussy.

The second time lasted a lot longer than the blow job and as soon as I came Tanya grabbed a pillow and stuffed it under her butt to elevate herself so my sperm could flow down into her. Looking at her lying there with her pussy pushed up like that made my soft cock start to harden and as I slipped into her for the second time I was hoping that it wouldn't take so I could come back and do it again. The second time she clawed at me, bit my shoulder and begged me to fuck her hard and I was sweating bullets when I finally came. Once more she stuffed the pillow under her ass when I pulled out of her and then she said:

"In my mouth Rob, put it in my mouth so I can get you up again."

I did Tanya one more time before I left to go home and just before she let me out the front door, she kissed me and thanked me for what I'd just done.

"I'd like to do it every day until I get pregnant, but Tom is used to making love three or four times a week and even though he is okay with this I won't give him sloppy seconds. Call me tomorrow, okay?"

I thought about what had just happened all the way home and as I pulled into the driveway it occurred to me that if Peg was having me watched she would find out about my visits to Tom and Tanya's and notice that Tom left, but that I stayed for several hours after. The next morning I called Tanya and explained my thoughts to her, but she told me not to worry, that no one would see Tom leave because he didn't; he went down to his basement workshop and stayed there until I left."

That information gave me pause. It was one thing to make love to Tanya when Tom was gone, but could I do it if I knew he was in the house? Tanya must have known what I was thinking because she said:

"Don't worry Rob; it will be okay. I promise."

That afternoon I got a call from Tom asking me to have a drink with him after work. Talk about awkward. Try sitting down with a guy you have known for twenty years, who is a good friend and whose wife you have just screwed with his knowledge. He must have known what I was thinking so he cut right to it.

"I know this is awkward for you Rob; hell buddy, it is awkward for me, but I have to talk with you about the situation we are in. First off, and I told you this when I left you and Tanya alone, I am 100% okay with it. I mean that Rob, but that said I have to tell you that Tanya didn't tell you the full truth. I know she told you about wanting a child and about me being sterile, but I also know that she didn't tell you the rest of it. To be blunt about it buddy - I can't get it up! I haven't been able to make love to Tanya in over a year."

My God! That is why she was so hot last night; she was playing catch up. And her telling me that she didn't want to give Tom sloppy seconds was her way of covering for his inability. She didn't want me to know he was impotent because she didn't want me to think less of him as a man. Not that I would have, but she didn't know that. What a difference between her and Peg. Tanya put Tom first, even in difficult circumstances while Peg thought only of herself.

"I don't know if it came through to you last night," Tom went on, "but Tanya is an extremely sexual person. My not being able to perform was driving her up the wall. She has tried hard to hold it together Rob, but sooner or later she was going to cheat on me. I know that seems harsh, but that is what would happen. I know she loves me and that she would do her best to hide her cheating from me, but I would know. How could I not? If she got laid she wouldn't be climbing walls anymore and I would notice.

"I love her Rob; the woman is my life. If I didn't have her I would just die and that's the problem. If she snuck off and cheated behind my back I couldn't live with her. I would know why she did it and I would understand why she did it, but I couldn't live with the dishonesty of it. The only solution, at least as far as I could see, was to make it happen out in the open, but Tanya isn't the kind of woman who would agree to taking a lover and going into the bedroom while I sat in the living room and watched TV while she fucked. She could probably have done it with a stranger in a motel room with me not knowing, but she couldn't just do a guy with me knowing and then a different guy the following week and another the week after that. What we needed was someone steady, someone we both liked and were comfortable with.

"We sat down and made a list of possible candidates, but couldn't agree on anyone. We kept coming back to you, but we were afraid that if we started with you and then Peg came back home it would stop and we would have to start back over. And Peg would eventually come back to you. Everyone who knows Adam White knows that he is a dip-shit asshole and Peg would soon find out and go home to you secure in the knowledge that you had no idea of what she had been doing. I have no idea why she thinks you are that dumb. I can only guess that she thinks you love her so much that the thought would never occur to you that she might be up to something."

I had to chuckle at that. "She pretty much read me right because that is just the way it went and it was only because the separation was dragging on and on that I finally tumbled to the fact that something wasn't kosher."

"Well, you do know now and I know, even if Peg doesn't, that now that you do know, she is history. I know you won't take her back now under any conditions. That freed Tanya and me up so that we could approach you. Tanya and I want a child Rob, and Tanya needs a steady sex life, and until the doctors can find and fix my problem someone else is going to have to provide that sex life for her. I know it sounds silly to say this, but you making love to my wife is going to save my marriage. You just have to get comfortable with the idea that I know and that I'm all right with it."

I didn't know what to say. The whole thing was so off the wall that even though it had already happened once, I was still having trouble believing it. Tom stared down into his drink and then looked up at me and said:

"It kills me not to be able to take care of my wife Rob, but it would kill me if I lost her. I need you to do this for me bud, I really do. Can I count on you?"

I stared at him for a few seconds and then nodded my head yes.

***

Sunday I had Tom, Tanya and three other couples over for a barbecue and when the other couples had gone, Tom went into the den and played on my computer while Tanya and I went up to my bedroom. By the time I was undressed, Tanya was lying on the bed, legs spread wide and imploring me to hurry. I got on the bed and lowered my head down her pussy and she cried:

"No baby, no need for that, no need for that because I'm already hot and I need it."

"My house Tanya, and in my house and on my bed we do it my way."

I lowered my mouth to her cunt and then using my tongue, I attacked her engorged clit. Then I slid a finger inside her and started working it. She moaned and I added a second finger. I started moving my fingers faster all the while staying on her clit with my mouth. She cried out several times and then her hands grabbed the back of my head and gripped it hard as she had a long explosive orgasm. I kept my mouth on her pussy until her tremors subsided and then I pulled back from her.

"Sweet Jesus baby, that was amazing, but I want your cock now. Hurry baby, hurry."

I moved up, lifted her legs onto my shoulders and slid my cock into her with one steady push. "Oh God," she moaned as my pubic bone hit hers and then I fucked her! I did not make love, I fucked! She groaned with pleasure as I drove my hard cock into her, pulled back, and then drove in hard again. Her legs came up and locked on me and her hands clutched my ass. Her nails dug into me as she tried to pull me even deeper into her. For several minutes, I pounded into her as hard and as fast as I could and then I felt her body tremble as she had another orgasm. Her pussy sucked at my cock, squeezed it like she had a third hand inside her cunt and I erupted. I pumped shot after shot of sperm deep into her and then I held myself still until my cock went limp and then I pulled out.

I kept her legs up on my shoulders so gravity would help my little guys in their race to her core in search of her egg. After maybe thirty seconds, I told her to put a pillow under her butt and then I let her legs down. Tanya looked up at me and said:

"Peg walked away from this? The woman must be crazy or stupid."

With that stroke to my ego, I just had to justify it so I swung over her in a sixty-nine and as she said, "No Rob, I need it to do its job." I laughed and said, "If any is still there around the opening it isn't going anywhere anyway" and I buried my face in her pussy. Seconds later her mouth closed around my cock and five minutes after that I was driving deep into her for the second time.

I saw that Tom knew what he was talking about when he said that Tanya was a very sexual person. She got a third time out of me before I walked her and Tom to their car. Tom shook my hand and Tanya kissed me on the cheek and we all agreed that the day had been a success and that we should do it again sometime soon. Anyone watching would assume that we were talking about the barbecue.

***

Monday afternoon I met with John Abbott from the Corliss agency and as he handed me the report he said, "I'm sorry. Every time I do one of these things I hope it is all a simple misunderstanding and that nothing is going on, but there is no doubt here. Your fee also covers our court appearance on your behalf if what you decide to do goes to trial."

I shook his hand and left his office and on the drive home, I wasn't near as enraged as I thought I would be. It was probably because I had already accepted that it was true and that by the time I got the report I had settled everything in my mind. What was I going to do about the situation? Nothing that I had not already done. The only thing left for me to do was time the draw on the house line of credit so Peg wouldn't know about it until it was too late. I would see an attorney and get the papers drawn up, but I would hold off on having them served until I was ready.

***

For the next five weeks, I saw Tom and Tanya three or four times a week either at their house or mine. They let the word out that I was going through a rough patch and that they were spending time with me trying to cheer me up. I got my weekly phone call from Peg, but I stopped asking her how she was and when she would be coming home.

Finally I'd had enough. I wrote checks against the line of credit and as soon as they cleared I found an apartment, moved out of the house and had Peg served with the divorce papers. They cited "irreconcilable differences" instead of adultery. I did it that way so that Peg wouldn't know that I knew about White. She would see it as my way of trying to push her into deciding to come home. She would call me, feed me a line of bullshit about how I was over-reacting and then she would probably suggest that we meet someplace for a drink and to have dinner where she would try and calm me down and "talk some sense" into me. I would agree to meet her, listen to her and then tell her I would think about it. It would buy me several days for the line of credit checks to clear and for me to clean out the checking and savings accounts.

It went just how I thought it would. First the phone call telling me that I was being unreasonable; that there was no need for me to get attorneys involved. I told her that I was tired of the 'neither fish nor fowl' situation.

"You don't want to be with me so it is time for me to accept it and move on with my life."

I agreed to meet her at Angelo's. It was the first time I'd seen her since she walked out on me and she looked good. I was going to miss her - strike that, I did miss her - since it was obvious to me that I did still love her, but even if she came back to me I knew that there was no way I could ever live with her again. I didn't tell her that though; instead I sat there and listened to her as she fed me a line of bull-shit. She was seeing an analyst and she was helping Peg understand blah, blah, blah and Peg was making good progress and all she needed was a little more time.

"I know it is hard on you baby, but it is just as hard on me. Please baby, please; just a little more time."

I told her I would think on it and let her know. I waited two days and then I called my attorney and told him it was time to go to step two. He quashed the divorce papers and sent Peg a notice that the filing had been cancelled. I got a call from Peg at work thanking me and telling me that I wouldn't regret it. I smiled knowing that I didn't regret it, but that she didn't know why. But she would soon find out.

That night I had dinner at Tom and Tanya's and after dinner Tanya and I retired to her bedroom and as Tanya spread herself for me she said:

"Can we make love tonight instead of fucking? I'd like to make love to the father of my child."

"Are you sure?"

"Positive. The home test told me Tuesday and the doctor confirmed it this afternoon. You are going to be a daddy."

We only did it once that night, but it was a long, slow and very satisfying session. When it was over I told her it might be a while before I saw her again.

"I'm going to end the farce with Peg and White this week and I may have to leave town for a while."

"Don't do anything too drastic lover; I am going to need the father of my baby to be around."

"That would be Tom sweetie. You need to start thinking like that."

"You know what I mean lover. Just because I'm bred doesn't

mean I'm not going to need you anymore."

***

Adam White was a member of the Fraternal Order of Eagles and since he had been elected Sergeant at Arms he had never missed a meeting. He left that Wednesday's meeting in a good mood as after talking to several of the more influential members he believed he had a shot if he ran for higher office in the order. He was in that good mood when he got out of his car in the parking lot of his condo. He locked his car door, turned, and felt a blinding pain before everything turned black.

He was found by a neighbor who called 911 and the paramedics who responded to the call rushed him to the emergency room at the hospital where it was found that both of his arms and both of his legs had been broken and there was damage to his genital area so severe that both of his testicles had to be removed. He was in great pain when he opened his eyes and saw he was in a hospital room and discovered that he couldn't move. He had casts on his arms and legs and was in traction. He saw Peggy standing next to his bed with a horrified expression on her face before he faded out again.

I wasn't there when it happened of course, but I received a full description of what occurred when the man walked into the room, walked over to Peg who was standing next to the bed and looking down at White. The man asked her if she was Margaret Olson and when she said yes he handed her some papers and told her she had been served. She looked confused as she opened the envelope and saw that she was being sued for divorce only this time the grounds were infidelity. She looked at the word "infidelity" and then at the wreck lying on the bed in front of her and her face lost all of its color and took on a horrified expression as she understood what it meant. She moaned, "Oh my God" and then she sat down on a chair and started crying.

I stuck around long enough for the police to ask me where I was that night. It turns out that I was at a poker game that started an hour before the Eagles meeting and lasted until an hour after White was admitted to the hospital. Peg paid for my alibi although she didn't know it. The guys were on my side and would have done it for free, but the object of the exercise was to stick it to Peg so I used her credit to show my appreciation. Home Shopping Network took her Visa card number for the digital cameras that I gave Bill and Steve. E-bay charged her MasterCard for the laptop I gave Mike and the 19" flat screen monitor that I gave Phil. She even paid for the aluminum ball bat.

I had six weeks of vacation and three weeks of comp time coming to me and I took a two month leave of absence in conjunction with that time and when the police were satisfied that I had nothing to do with White's misfortune, that they could prove anyway, I made arrangements to leave town and take a fishing trip down in Mexico.

Before I left I told my attorney not to push the divorce and just let it lay there until Peg started fighting it and then drop it. We would stay married, but I would have nothing to do with her.

I called Tom and Tanya once a week to see how things were going and they told me that Peg had moved back into the house and as far as anyone could tell "true love" must not have been in the cards for Peg and White because she never went back to visit him after the day she was served while standing next to his hospital bed.

The maxed out credit card bills must have started hitting the mailbox and she must have found out that the savings and checking accounts were dry, the line of credit was pegged out and that the CDs in the bank deposit box were fake because the next word I got was that Peg was frantically trying to find me and no one could tell her where I was. My boss, who knew the full story, told her I was gone when she called him, trying to find me. He told her that I just came in one day, said I was leaving and asked for my check. Basically what he did was lead her to believe that I had quit without notice. He didn't tell her that but he did lead her to believe it.

A call to my attorney demanding that he set up a meeting with me got her the information that I had dropped the divorce action, paid him off and that he no longer represented me. She had no choice. Four months after I had left on my fishing trip she filed bankruptcy. She ended up losing the house and she had to give up her Lexus and start driving a used Geo. Once I heard that I came back from Mexico, got an apartment on the other side of town from where Peg lived and did my best to stay away from places where she might see me.

Tanya was five months pregnant and looking sexier than any woman had a right to look and we picked up where we left off. This time though we didn't have to worry about whether or not someone was keeping tabs on me and two or three times a week she spent the night at my place or I spent the night at hers.

I was back two months before Peg found out and one day when I got off work I found her waiting in the parking lot for me. She got out of her car and headed for me, but I ignored her, got in my car and pulled out of the lot. In the rear view I saw her hurry to her car and I slowed down so she would be able to keep me in sight. I'd have it out with her, but not in the parking lot at work. I kept my speed where she would have no trouble following me and about ten minutes later I pulled into the lot at Bud's Bar and Grill.

I was inside by the time she got parked and I was sitting at the bar ordering a Bud Light when she came in, looked around, saw me and headed toward me. She was already mouthing off as she approached:

"Don't think you can run from me you bastard."

I know Peg and so I knew what she would do and I spun around on the stool and caught her wrist as she swung at my head. I squeezed as hard as I could and she gasped in pain as I said:

"I have every reason in the world to want to hurt you Peg, so best you don't push me too far. You keep your hands to yourself unless you want to feel some real pain."

I let go of her wrist and said, "I wasn't running from you. I drove nice and slow so you could follow me here. I wasn't going to air your dirty laundry in the parking lot where I work. It doesn't matter here because everyone here already knows you are a whore."

"I want to talk to you."

"I don't want to talk to you. I've already listened to enough of your lies."

"I want my money back."

"What money would that be Peg?"

"You owe me the money you took out against the house and half of everything else we had was mine and I want it."

"Well you ain't going to get it Peg. My position on the matter is that it was restitution for what you did to me. What is it the lawyers say when they sue? Compensation for pain and suffering and loss of conjugal rights? I figure what I got just about covers the pain and suffering I went through for going without sex for a year and a half while you were giving it away to someone else and for the humiliation I suffered as everyone that I knew looked on me as stupid cuckold."

"Damn you Rob, I lost my parents' home because of you."

"Big deal Peg; it couldn't have meant all that much to you since as I recall you moved out to shack up with another man."

"I mean it Rob; I want that money."

"Here is a newsflash for you Peggy; you will never get a dime of it from me. You tried to fuck over me and you got caught and I made you pay. Live with it."

"I guess we will just have to see what the courts say."

"Doesn't matter what they say Peg. Here is the way it will work. You will have to get a lawyer and sue me for divorce to get me into court so the court can issue an order as to the division of assets. As soon as you sue I will counter sue. A good lawyer can stall things for six to eight months and during that time you will be paying your lawyer. Can you afford to pay him to get nothing? I have all the evidence I need to fight you in court and if I win you will take it in the ass. Worst case scenario for me is that I'm ordered to split the assets. I say "okay judge" and leave the court.

"You and your lawyer wait and wait and wait for the money, but the money never comes. You call me, but I don't take your calls so your lawyer, who you are still paying, goes back to court and gets a court order telling me to pay by such and such time. You and the lawyer wait and wait and when the deadline arrives you still haven't gotten a dime from me.

"Your lawyer, still billing you for his time, goes back to court and gets a judgment against me. I have no savings or checking accounts that can be attached. My car is a lease so nothing for you there. I live in a furnished apartment so there isn't anything there you can get. All you can do with your judgment is garnish my wages and the first time that I get a paycheck that has been garnished, I will quit my job. So what do we have here Peg? A good year's worth of lawyer's fees out of your pocket and all for maybe two hundred dollars out of one paycheck.

"All that's left for you to try is to go back to the judge and get him to threaten me with going to jail for contempt of court if I don't comply with his orders. All that will get you Peg is a post card from me from some small fishing village in Mexico where I will take up residence until my money runs out. And I've got a lot Peg, thanks to you. Face it Peggy. You fucked over me, got caught and I got even. Consider yourself fortunate. Think about what happened to your boyfriend and consider yourself very fortunate. He lost his balls and now he can never fuck with another man's wife. You, on the other hand, can still spread for anyone you want."

"I knew it! I knew you had something to do with what happened to Adam."

"What you think you know and what you can prove are two very different things Peg. By the way, how are things going with your love affair? From what I hear you haven't seen the poor man since his first day in the hospital."

"What would be the point? You took away the only thing he had going for him."

"Oh that's cold Peg, even for you."

"It's the truth. He was extremely well endowed and he was a marvelous lover, but I would have tired of him eventually and come home."

"Oh gee Peg; if only I had known. All of the unpleasantness could have been avoided if I had but known that someday you would have come home to me. Oh damn! I guess by my actions I messed that up didn't I? I'll have to carry that regret to my grave. Oh what a joy life could have been had we only communicated better."

"You can be such an asshole."

"Yes Peg and you are a worthless, cheating whore."

I finished my beer, got up and said, "Have a rotten life Peg" and I left the bar.

Three days later I was served with divorce papers citing irreconcilable differences. I didn't contest it and she was awarded half of the marital assets and I was ordered to pay her the money borrowed against the line of credit. I wished her luck in getting anything and tossed the final decree in the trash. She must have believed me when I told her how things would go because I never heard from her again.

One interesting thing came out of the mess. Everyone agreed that White was a dip-shit asshole, but even dip-shit assholes can have a friend or two and one of White's was Peggy's boss. He wasn't happy with the way she treated White after his misfortune and he fired her. Well, fired isn't the way it was put. A downturn in the economy necessitated a downsizing and Peggy was let go, but everyone knew that she was fired. She couldn't find work in our area so she relocated to California where she had some relatives and no one - not even her sister - has heard from her since.

***

There is one more chapter to the story. It was a sad ending, but at the same time a glorious beginning.

Tanya had a beautiful baby girl and Tom doted on her and spoiled her rotten. Uncle Rob was a constant visitor and spent many, many hours crawling around on the floor with little Martha.

Tom never told Tanya or me the full story. He knew why he had erectile dysfunction, but he hid it from Tanya. He had cancer and it didn't get caught in time and the cancer spread. Following his funeral Tanya handed me an envelope addressed to me. It was addressed to me and written across the front of the envelope were the words, "For Rob's eyes only." I looked at her and she shrugged and said,

"I have no idea. It is addressed to you so I haven't seen what's inside."

I opened it and read:

"Hey bud; if you are reading this I'm gone. There was a reason I picked you (yes, it was me, not Tanya) to father our child. I knew I wouldn't be there for them and I wanted someone I knew I could trust to be around to watch over them. I knew I could count on you so you got elected. Don't let me down bud; take good care of our girls."

T

I handed the letter to Tanya and she read it and started crying. I took her in my arms to comfort her and when she was all cried out she asked me what I was going to do.

"I'm going to do just what he knew I would do; I'm going to take care of my girls."

Six months later Tanya and I were married.

End of the 7th Story

The Ex Wants a Favor

The doorbell rang and I opened the door to find Willy standing there.

"What the fuck do you want?"

"To talk. To clear the air so to speak."

"I don't need to hear anything that you have to say."

"Maybe not, but I need to say it. It won't take long. May I come in?"

I stared at her for several minutes (looking mostly at her throat and wanting to put my hands around it and squeeze as hard as I could) before stepping aside and letting her come in. She went straight for the kitchen and I followed along behind her. She pulled out a chair and sat down and I took the chair opposite.

"How have you been?" she asked.

"How the fuck do you think I've been after the hell you put me through?"

"Yes, well, that's why I'm here Rob. To apologize."

"Like that will help any."

"You aren't making this easy Rob."

"I don't have to Willy; I didn't invite you over."

As I sat there and looked across the table at her, my mind flashed back.

***

I met Wilhelmina at a frat party during my junior year at State. She was the date of one of my frat brothers and as soon as I laid eyes on her I thought "lucky bastard." I won't say that it was love at first sight, but I was certainly taken with her. I couldn't take my eyes off of her and of course she noticed it.

When the party started to break up and just before she left she handed me a piece of paper and said "Call me" and then she was gone. I looked at the paper, saw that it was a phone number and then I sighed and dropped it in the waste basket.

It was a week later - to the day - when I saw her again. I was downtown having lunch at a small café when someone sat down across from me. I looked up and saw that it was Wilhelmina.

"You didn't call." I shrugged and she said, "I must be losing my touch. I kind of expected my phone to be ringing the next morning before I was even out of bed. You seemed interested. Every time I looked your way you were watching me. What happened to the interest?"

"It is a guy thing."

"A guy thing? Care to explain?"

"You were dating a fraternity brother and that made you off limits to me."

"Oh my, an honorable man. What a rarity in this day and age. For your information I was not dating Chad. Chad is my cousin and he took me to that frat party because I was curious as to what a frat party would be like."

She pulled out a pen and a note pad from her purse, wrote something on the pad and then tore off the sheet.

"I have to get back to work so let's try this again." She slid the piece of paper across the table to me and said, "Call me" and then she was up and gone. I called her that evening and we made a date. We started keeping company and three months after I graduated we were married.

Fast forward twenty-two years and three children later and I was sitting in my office at work when my secretary buzzed me and told me that there was a Mr. Sam Halley there to see me and I told her to send him in. When he came in he asked me if I was Robert Severs and as I said yes I was thinking "What an odd question. He was there to see me so why did he ask me if I was me? He took an envelope from his pocket and handed it to me and when I took it he said:

"You have been served."

He turned and walked out of my office. I opened the envelope and found out that Willy was suing me for divorce on the grounds of irreconcilable differences. To say that it came as a shock to me would be a massive understatement. As far as I had known, Willy and I had a great marriage. I had certainly not noticed anything wrong. She had seemed loving and affectionate. I thought our love life was a little better than adequate. We hadn't had major arguments or disagreements in the last couple of years. It did not make a whole lot of sense to me.

Then I read the second piece of paper in the envelope. It was a restraining order telling me that I could not come within 500 feet of Willy, my children or my home and that I was not to try and contact them without someone authorized by the court being present. The divorce paperwork upset me, but the restraining order pissed me off.

I called Dave, our in house attorney, and asked him if he could recommend a good divorce attorney and when he gave me a name I called the man. It turned out that the man had been a classmate of

Dave's and was also a close personal friend and when I called him for an appointment I was told that Dave had already called and paved the way for me. I was told to come right on down. As soon as I hung up, I got on the phone and cancelled all of our credit cards except for the Visa and American Express cards that were in my name only.

I told my secretary that I was leaving and might be gone for the rest of the day and then I headed for the lawyer's office. On the way I stopped at the bank and cleaned out all of our accounts and emptied the safe deposit box. I had several friends who had gone through divorces and I knew how things worked and I wasn't about to fuck around and try to talk to Wilhelmina to find out what was going on which would give her time to run up the credit cards with cash advances and get everything out of the bank before I could get to it. Actually I was surprised that Willy hadn't already beaten me to the bank, but I guess she must have miscalculated. I saw her pulling into the bank parking lot as I was sitting in my car getting ready to leave.

Andy, the attorney Dave had set me up with, read the paperwork I'd been served with and said:

"Pretty much boilerplate. Custody of the children, child support, separate maintenance and the right to maintain the home. And you say you never saw it coming?"

"Didn't have a clue."

"Have you done anything to set your wife against you? An affair or something like that?"

"Not a thing. I've had plenty of opportunities, but I kept my pants zipped. Hell, I had all that a man could want at home. Why stray and take a chance on screwing it up?"

"Well, if it wasn't something that you did it must be something that she is doing or has done. Would you have any objection to my putting someone on her to check her out?"

"None at all, but right now my major concern is getting into the house and getting my stuff out and getting that bullshit restraining order changed so I can at least talk to my kids."

"No problem there. I'll need to make some phone calls, but I am pretty sure that we can get you in the house this evening, but the restraining order may take a while. We have no idea what she is claiming as the reason to keep you away from them."

"Doesn't it matter that Chris is nineteen and Dave is eighteen? Aren't they considered adults? Angie is only sixteen so I know she isn't considered an adult, but the boys? How can she keep me away from them when they are old enough to go out on their own?"

"Again, I have no idea until I look into it. I'll give you a call later this afternoon."

I left his office feeling a little more in control and went back to my office. Andy called me at ten after four and told me that he would meet me at the house at six and that he would have someone from the court with him.

"He will inventory everything you remove from the house so be very careful not to take anything that your wife is likely to fight you over. If you must then you must, but be aware of the problems that it might cause. I saw one divorce drag on for months over a coffee table. Also, I contacted your wife's attorney and let him know we would be there in case he also wanted to monitor things."

"What about Willy?"

"Willy?"

"My wife, Wilhelmina."

"Her lawyer knows we will be there and I assume that he will inform her. She may choose to be there or not. I've also requested that the children be there, but whether that will happen, or not I don't know. I haven't had time to get a court order for a court supervised visit, but I kind of let your wife's attorney know that you are amicable to a quick resolution of the matter and his getting the children there as a show of good faith would go a long way toward speeding things up."

"I don't know that I want to speed things up. What I want is to know why."

"True, but what the other side doesn't know won't hurt us. He did tell me that he expected you to return what you took out of the checking and savings accounts before he found it necessary to petition the court."

"No. I'm not going to do anything that will make it easy on her."

"The court will order you to do it."

"Until they do she can stand on a street corner and beg for food."

"I can't tell you what to do, I can only advise, but you will lose this one."

"Yeah, but she will be nervous as hell and suffer until it happens."

***

Andy and a deputy sheriff were waiting when I got to what used to be my home with a rented trailer and two friends to help carry the large things.

"If your wife and children are inside, don't say a word to them. I'll do all the talking. Can you handle that?"

"I'm paying you for your expertise so I'll do whatever you say."

"Good. Okay, let's get it done."

Willy and the kids were there and so was a man that I assumed was either her attorney or someone on her attorney's staff. I told the deputy what I was taking and he started recording things on a clipboard as me and my friends started carrying them out to the trailer. Chris started to say something to me and Willy told him to be quiet. Apparently Andy had been expecting it and waiting for it. He opened his briefcase and said:

"Your father is under a court order not to contact you, but I expect that I can get that order changed at least as far as you two boys are concerned since you are both over eighteen. I may not be successful in your case Angie, but I will try. The court order forbids your father from contacting you, but says nothing about your initiating contact with him."

He took three cell phones out of his briefcase and handed one to each of the kids:

"Your father does not have the numbers to these phones so he cannot call you, but his office and cell phone numbers are preset in the phones. You may call him and talk to him as often as you like. The bills will come to my office and I will make copies available to the court to show that the calls are strictly one way."

"Can he do that?" Willy asked the man with her and he told her he wasn't sure and that he would have to look into it.

"Well until you do there will be no damned calls." She turned to the kids and said, "Give me those phones."

Dave put his phone in his pocket and said, "No. I don't know how you managed to get a judge to let you cut me off from dad, but I'm not going along with it."

"That goes for me too," Chris said as he put his phone in his shirt pocket.

"As long as you are living in this house you will do as ..."

"I'm over eighteen mom, and I can walk out of this house and there is nothing you can do about it."

"Same goes for me," Dave said.

I saw the slow burn come over Willy's face and I almost smiled. She turned to Angie and said:

"You aren't over eighteen. Give me that phone."

Angie tossed it to her and said, "No biggie. When I want to talk to dad I'm sure one of my big brothers will let me use a phone."

I left the house feeling pretty good about my kids at least.

"Thanks Andy. I loved seeing that shell shocked look on her face when you hit her with that phone gambit."

"It was a little dramatic and it wasn't really needed except for maybe Angie. I'm sure that what happened was just some bureaucratic paper shuffling. I'm betting that no one at the court even read the request for restraint since it is an almost common occurrence in divorce cases. If anyone had read it and noticed the ages of the two boys the paperwork would have been kicked back to your wife's attorney for revising. I'm pretty sure I can get it set aside tomorrow."

I thanked him for his quick response in getting me into the house and he told me he would call me the next day when he knew more.

***

I moved everything I'd removed from the house into a rented storage unit and then checked myself into a hotel close to work. The next morning I told my boss of my situation and asked for a couple of days off to look for an apartment and situate myself and he approved the time off. I found a nice two bedroom ten minutes from work. It had a pool and an exercise room and was within walking distance of several restaurants and stores. I signed a six month least and set about moving in.

I was moving in the bedroom set that I had taken out of my old home when Chris called me on my cell and asked me just what was going on. I told him that I didn't have a clue that his mother had hit me with it right out of the blue.

"She says she caught you cheating on her."

I was stunned! I had never been unfaithful to Willy and I told Chris that and then I asked him to try and get a little more information from his mother as the restraining order prevented me from talking to her.

At eleven, Andy called me and told me he had gotten the restraining order quashed as it pertained to the kids, but that it was still in effect as far as Wilhelmina and the house were concerned.

I heard from both Dave and Angie before the day was over and they told me the same thing that Chris had - that their mother said that I was cheating on her and she caught me. Any thought that I might have had about working things out with Willy were dashed when they told me that. The bitch was trying to poison my kids against me and I would never forgive her for that.

Three days later, Andy called me. "I put an investigator on your wife the first day you came to see me and I think we have the answer. Your wife is having an affair with a man she works with. From what he has been able to find out so far, it has been going on pretty hot and heavy for about six months. She probably decided that it was time to move you out so she could move him in. I think we should counter sue on grounds of infidelity."

"No, I don't want that. That would only slow the divorce down. If she has a lover I don't want her back. In fact, I don't want anything to do with her anymore. Just get me the best deal you can and get it over with."

"I'd like to keep the investigator on her for a little while more and get some hard evidence. It might come in useful later as leverage."

"Do it."

***

The divorce took on a life of its own. Chris couldn't get any more out of his mother other than "she knew" I was cheating. She told the kids that as long as "they lived under her roof" they were not to see me or talk to me. In response to that both Chris and Dave moved out and took up dormitory living at college.

Six weeks into the divorce, Angie called me and told me that her mother had moved a man into the house and into what had been our bedroom.

"I'm not staying here Daddy. I'll run away if I have to. But I'm not staying here."

I gave her Andy's number and told her to call him and then I called Andy and told him what was going on and he said he would take care of it. The next day Child Protection Services removed Angie from Wilhelmina's "care." They kept her for three days and then she was "placed" with me pending the custody portion of the divorce hearing.

My next call from Andy concerned the house. "Your wife's attorney just called. There is no money in the accounts so your wife can't make the house payment. It falls on you to do it."

"Call him back and tell him I'm not making any payments to

keep a roof over Wilhelmina's boyfriend's head. Tell him to tell my wife that since she has moved her lover into the house he can make the payment."

"You are being a little short sighted here. The house is an asset and when the divorce is final you will be entitled to half the value of the equity. If you don't make the payments and your wife can't you could lose the house to foreclosure."

"Yep, and Wilhelmina won't get a penny.

"You do realize that you could be held in contempt of court don't you? The court did order you to maintain the residence in the original court order."

"Yes, but that was so my family wouldn't be disrupted, but all three kids are out of the house now and that changes things."

"It is still a valid court order. It is my duty as your attorney to advise you that you do have to follow the orders of the court."

"What are they going to do to me if I don't, hold me in contempt? So what? All they can do if they hold me in contempt is throw me in jail until I agree to do what they say. If I go to jail I'll lose my job and there goes Willy's chance for separate maintenance. Hey! She will be working and I won't. Maybe she will have to pay me alimony. No Andy, tell her lawyer I don't pay a dime on that house as long as her boyfriend lives there with her."

***

After months of bullshit", the divorce finally was final. The day we signed the papers, Wilhelmina asked for five minutes alone with me. I hadn't said one word to her since the day I was served so I figured what the hell, why not.

She sat down on the other side of the conference table and then she smirked at me and asked:

"Well Rob, was she worth it?"

"Was who worth what?"

"Was your affair with Helen worth all that you have been through the last several months and all that you have lost?"

"What affair?"

"Oh come on Rob, I caught you red-handed."

"I have no idea what you are talking about."

"Deny it all you want Rob, but I saw it with my own eyes."

"I don't have a clue as to what you are talking about Wilhelmina and if babble is all you have for me we are done here" and I got up to leave.

"It was your birthday Rob and I came down to your office to surprise you and take you to lunch, but I was the one who was surprised. I saw you in your office with your arms around Helen and her head tucked into your shoulder. You were so wrapped up in each other that you didn't even notice me. I made up my mind right then and there to take a lover of my own and make you suffer. So Rob, was Helen worth it?"

I sat there and stared at her for maybe ten seconds and then said:

"My birthday. That would be the day that Helen's mother called her and told her that her father had just been killed in an accident. That would be the day that I held her and tried to comfort her as she cried into my shoulder while we waited for her husband to come down and pick her up. I never realized that you were so stupid Wilhelmina. All you had to do was knock lightly on the door to get my attention and I would have waved you in and then you would have known what was going on. Failing that you could have asked for an explanation when I got home that night. But you couldn't do anything normal and sensible like that could you? You had to run off half-cocked and be stupid.

"Let me ask you the same question Wilhelmina. Your children don't want anything to do with you; everything you had is now gone - sold off to meet the conditions of the asset split - and the man who used to worship the ground you walked on now hates your guts. Tell me Wilhelmina, was it worth it?"

I got up and left her sitting at the table.

Angie ended up with me and the court ordered a fifty - fifty split of the assets. The alimony issue was dropped when Andy informed Willy's lawyer that we were going to counter sue on grounds of infidelity and that would drag things on forever and let Willy's family know what she had been doing.

Three months after the divorce, Willy married her boyfriend and now here she was - one year later - sitting across the table from me and telling me that she wanted to apologize.

***

I sat there and stared at her and waited for her to go on.

"I was wrong Rob. You were absolutely right. I was stupid and I did go off and behave like a bull in a china shop, but I was hurt Rob - really hurt - and I wasn't thinking straight. I took up with Hal to get even with you. I only meant to see him for a while and then rub your nose in it, tell you we were now even and then ask you if you wanted to try and make the marriage work or call it quits. I stupidly listened to Hal when he said the thing to do was file for divorce. That way you would have to crawl to me and beg for forgiveness and I would be in the driver's seat without you ever having to know about Hal. It didn't work out that way. I found out later that was Hal's plan all along. He wanted to marry me and he figured the divorce would drive you away. He was right - it did."

"Water under the bridge Willy. Okay, you've said you're sorry; you can go now."

"We had twenty-one good years together Rob. Can't you be a little nicer than that?"

"No Willy, you burned the nice out of me."

She was silent for several seconds and then she said, "I have another reason for being here besides apologizing."

"What?"

"I miss my babies Rob, but they won't have anything to do with me. I thought if I could at least get on friendly terms with you and they saw it they might at least talk to me."

"So the apology is bogus?"

"No rob, the apology is genuine. I am truly sorry for what I've done to you and the family. I don't know how I can make it up to you, but if there is any way, any way at all to do it I will. But even though you hate me I'm hoping that you will help me at least get to where the kids will talk to me."

"I don't know Wilhelmina. We don't talk about you so I have no idea if they will be open to having anything to do with you. I've never bad mouthed you to them other than to finally tell them why you did what you did, but when you moved your boyfriend into the house only weeks after you kicked me out you poisoned them against you. I don't know if my acting friendly with you will change the way they feel."

"I have to try something Rob. I know you don't owe me anything, but I'm asking you to please help me get back in touch with my babies."

I could not have cared less about her healing the rift between her and the kids. She had made her bed so let her lie in it. I enjoyed seeing her suffering, but as I sat there feeling good about her feeling bad, I had an idea. I didn't know if I could pull it off, but I could try and if it worked it would warm my heart for years and years to come.

"I'll see what I can do," I told her, "but it won't be all that easy. We will have to pretend that we are a lot more affectionate toward each other than we are. By that I mean it will have to look to the kids like we really have let bygones be bygones. It will mean things like kisses on the cheek and hugs and things like that. It won't be all that easy for me to pretend, can you?"

"It won't be hard for me Rob. I realized way too late how much I loved you. There hasn't been a day since the divorce was final that I haven't thought of you, what we had and what I threw away."

***

To make the long story shorter, Willy and I found reasons to be together when the kids would be around to see us and as the kids saw us seem to draw closer and closer, they came around and Willy got back on good terms with her children.

As we spent more time together, Willy started treating me like her best friend and confidant. Maybe three months after we started the charade for the kids she confided in me that her husband wasn't all that great in bed. He was good at oral, but he lacked the stamina for good, hard sex. She admitted that she missed having me in her bed.

"That was your choice Willy. I didn't leave your bed; you pushed me out of it."

"Since it was me that pushed you out, could I pull you back in?"

"Why on Earth would you want to do that Willy?"

"I don't know why I just said that Rob. There are times I just get so confused. I miss you Rob."

I smiled inwardly as I thought to myself, "Enough to cheat on your husband?" but outwardly I said, "Well, for what it is worth Willy, I miss you too."

I left it at that and waited to see what she would do.

She started teasing me and I let her get away with it and the teasing got a little more blatant. She would tell me how much she missed my cock and I'd answer back that it was too bad she was married because I sure missed her pussy. Another time she told me that I was the best that she'd ever had in bed and I laughingly told her to lose her husband and then give me a call.

Then her husband went out of town for a week long training seminar and on the second night he was gone, Willy called me and asked me if I could come over to her place and have dinner with her.

"I'm lonely Rob, I'm not used to being alone."

"I'm sorry Willy, but I can't come over to your place. I'm expecting an important call and I can't leave."

"Maybe I could come over there?"

"Sure Willy, come on over."

Wilhelmina might be my ex-wife and I didn't like her a bit, but she was still the best piece of ass I'd ever had and I had been looking forward to what I expected to happen ever since I agreed to help her get back in touch with the kids. Half an hour after I hung up the phone, the doorbell rang and I opened the door to find Wilhelmina standing there looking like she was planning on getting fucked. She had on a short skirt, high heels and a fairly low cut blouse that obviously didn't have a bra under it. I led her into the kitchen, sat her down at the table and then poured her a glass of white wine.

"You do remember that wine makes me horny don't you?"

"That's why I ran out and bought six bottles when you said you were coming over."

She took a sip of her wine and said, "You did? You naughty boy you."

She was silent for a moment or so and then said, "Remember the time you told me to lose the husband and give you a call and you would come running?"

I nodded a yes.

"Could we not consider Hal being gone for a week as "losing" him?"

I sat and looked at her for a bit and then stood and offered her my hand. She rose and took it and I led her into the bedroom. We both stripped and then I said:

"You were the one who gave this cock up Willy. If you want it you have to ask for it."

"I want your cock Rob. I want to suck it, I want it in my pussy and I'm dying to have it slide into my ass. Give it to me baby. Fuck my brains out."

"Okay Willy, you get it in the order you asked. Mouth, pussy and then ass."

She smiled and then went to her knees and waited for me to walk over to her. I held my cock in my hand and stroked it and said, "You have to come over here and get it Willy."

She crawled across the floor and took me in her mouth. I let her suck on me for several minutes and then told her to get on the bed and spread her legs. As I moved between them she said:

"Give it to me hard Rob. I haven't had a decent fuck since the last time you and I did it."

"Hubby doesn't get the job done?"

"His idea of great sex is to push into me for two minutes, grunt, cum and then roll over and go to sleep. The only thing that makes sex bearable with him is that he is pretty good when it comes to eating pussy."

"So why did you marry such a dud?"

"I didn't know he was a dud until it was too late. I was having orgasms all over the place from the excitement of getting even with you. Cheating on you was such a turn on that I wasn't paying attention to the fact that it wasn't Hal giving me those orgasms. By the time I found out that you hadn't cheated on me it was too late. I was pregnant and I had to marry Hal.

"You have another kid?"

"No, I lost it, but by then I was already stuck with Hal. You going to talk or fuck me?"

"What do you want me to do Willy?"

"Put your cock in me and fuck my brains out. Do it like you used to and make me scream."

Like I said, she was the best piece of ass I'd ever had and she brought out the best in me. I fucked her and made her scream; went sixty-nine with her until I was hard again and then took her doggie style while she howled at me to push it deeper and fuck her harder. I came and she sucked me hard again and when she had me standing tall she said:

"My ass Rob; I want it in my ass."

I buried my cock in her shit chute and she moaned and cried and begged me to get her off:

"Make me cum baby, make me cum. Pound me and get me off baby."

I was so into making her cry and moan that I forgot that I needed to get her out of the house before Angie got home. In fact I forgot all about Angie until breakfast the next morning when she said:

"You and mom were sure noisy last night. Does it mean that you will be getting back together?"

All I could do was lie.

"We are working on it honey. I don't know if we can make it happen, but we are working on it."

***

I'm fucking Willy two or three times a week. Sometimes it is long lunch hours and sometimes it is the 'girl's night out' she tells Hal that she is having with the girls she works with. Sometimes it is a Saturday Avon party or a Sunday Mary Kay party. One thing that they all have in common is that they have all been captured on tape by the nanny-cams that I have hidden around my place. I have everything from the first night in my kitchen when she asked if we could consider Hal's trip as 'losing' him to last night's fuck-a-thon where I got her on tape telling me what a limp-dicked waste Hal is.

One of these days I am going to get tired of the bitch and I'll tell her to fuck off and when I do, I plan on sending all of the tapes I have to Hal along with a note that says something along the lines of:

"You fucked her when she was married to me so I have been fucking her while she is married to you. Makes us even, right?"

Sometimes revenge can be just so damned sweet!

End of the 8th Story

The Wedding, The Funeral

Foreword: I know that a lot of people think that the letters sent in to magazines such as Penthouse Letters are phony and are actually written by the magazine's staff. On that I can't say for sure one way or another. I do know that a lot of the letters sent in are fantasies and I also know for sure that when the magazine receives letters the editors change them for one reason or another. How do I know this? Because it has happened to me. In the fall of 1996 I sent a letter to Penthouse Letters that was published as The Letter of the Month in December 1996 under the title of Coming and Going. The letter had been changed so much that the original "flavor" had been lost. In fact, from my standpoint, they butchered it. I was doing a hard drive cleanup last week and I pulled up the original that I had sent in and thought it would be a kick to post it in its original form and see if anyone remembered it and could see the changes made by the Penthouse Letters staff. The title that I had originally given the story was The Wedding and The Funeral.

***

I'd led a pretty active sex life when I was in high school and as a result my reputation wasn't very good. Determined to turn things around, I made a vow that I was going to be a 'good girl' in college, stay away from boys and just earn my degree. It was a vow that lasted all of two months. Two months into the term, I met Henry and fell absolutely head-over-heels in love. Henry had, at least in my opinion, one major flaw - he was determined to remain a virgin until he married. No matter how hard I tried I could not get Henry to fuck me. I would give him hand jobs and blowjobs and when he got hot I would pull off my panties and try to mount him, but he would always push me away and tell me to be patient. As a result, I was always super horny and considerably frustrated. Several boys from my hometown, who had in the past shared my favors, were always sniffing around, but even though I was sorely tempted, I figured if Henry could wait until the wedding, so could I.

The day of our wedding, I was extremely antsy, wanting to get all the ceremonial bullshit out of the way so we could get to the bedroom, but with both family and friends all over the place we had to go through all the motions. By the time the reception was almost over I was hotter than a firecracker thanks to all the 'feels' I received while dancing with men who had at one time or another fucked me or been the recipients of either one of my blowjobs or hand jobs. One guy even cornered me on the way to the bathroom and asked me to kiss the head of his dick for old time's sake (after looking both ways to see if anyone was around, I did it). All of the attention, plus my eager expectation of finally getting fucked after a full year of going without, had me more than ready.

Fate has a way of fucking you over though and on that night fate got me good. It was time to leave the reception and Henry was falling down drunk. I don't mean 'tipsy', or 'mellowed out', I mean he was in a stupor. I had to get Charlie, the best man, and a couple of the guys who had been ushers to help me carry Henry up to our room. They dumped Henry on the bed and the ushers left while Charlie stayed to help me get Henry out of his clothes. We got him undressed and we were standing there looking down at him when Charlie turned to me and said:

"There is no way that a sexy lady like you should have to spend her wedding night without being made love to."

And with that, he put his arms around me and pulled me to him and kissed me on the lips. He caught me by surprise and while I didn't return the kiss, I didn't push him away either. His tongue probed my mouth as he gently turned me and bent me backwards and I suddenly found myself lying on the bed next to Henry with Charlie on top of me. Charlie had the fastest hands of any man I ever met because before I could push him away, he had my wedding dress up around my waist, the crotch of my panties pulled aside and at least two fingers in my pussy.

As his tongue worked in my mouth and his fingers probed my cunt, I tried to push him away and when he pulled his mouth off mine I told him to stop.

"We can't do this, it's not right. Please don't Charlie, please don…" but it was too late, for with one quick move he rolled just a little, the head of his cock touched my pussy lips and with one little shove - he was in. I kept saying, "No, we can't, we can't do this. It's not right, we can't" but of course we were doing it and by the time he had pushed into me four or five times I was starting to fuck back. I pulled my legs back until my knees were almost touching my ears and levered my pussy back up at him and took him in as deep as he would go. He hadn't plunged his cock into me more than a dozen times before I went into my first orgasm. I reached up and grabbed the cheeks of his ass with both hands and pulled him to me and started urging him on.

"Fuck me, fuck me, come on fuck me harder" and Charlie listened and obeyed.

He was pounding into me and I had forgotten all about Henry. The only thing I had on my mind was Charlie's beautiful cock as a second orgasm washed over me. I was making all kinds of noise by now, moaning, groaning, and begging Charlie to fuck me. I was thrashing around on the bed like a woman possessed (which I suppose I was) and I'm only surprised that I didn't dump us all on the floor. When I felt Charlie tense up and I knew he was going to cum, I tried to get him to slow down just a bit because I felt another orgasm building in me and I didn't want him to finish and leave me hanging, but he was too far gone and as he pumped his hot sperm into me I was crying "Don't cum baby, don't cum -stay with me - I'm almost there - hold on."

Charlie got up, bent over and kissed me and told me to hang on for a minute or so and then he got up and left. He was gone for two or three minutes and while I waited for him to come back, I masturbated myself and looked over at Henry - he hadn't moved.

When Charlie got back he walked up to me and put his cock in my face, "Get me hard baby, get me hard again."

I opened my mouth and went to work on it while still fingering myself. I had Charlie hard in less than two minutes and he wasted no time in getting me on my hands and knees and climbing on the bed behind me. I was already pushing back at him before his cock even touched me. Charlie proceeded to fuck me as hard as he could and in less time than it took to tell about it, I had my third orgasm of the night. Charlie slowed his strokes and I fell forward and as I lay there wondering whether or not to push my luck and let Charlie fuck me to another orgasm or to hustle him out the door, I felt him ease out of me and get off the bed. But in less than a minute he was back behind me and I felt him drive into me again. He started fucking me hard and fast and I wondered where he got all of his stamina.

Pretty soon I felt another orgasm coming on and I was driving back on his cock in frenzy when all of a sudden I felt something hit my cheek. I opened my eyes and saw a hard cock aimed at my mouth; it took a few seconds to register that there was a cock in my face at the same time a cock was pounding my pussy. I looked up and saw the cock in my face belonged to Tony, one of the ushers from the wedding, and a quick glance back behind me showed that George, another one of the ushers, owned the cock that was doing such a good job fucking me. That same backward glance saw that Charlie was sitting on the couch with two other guys from the wedding party. Charlie just smiled at me.

"Baby, you were so hot when I first fucked you that I knew I couldn't cool you down by myself."

I opened my mouth to protest and that gave Tony the opening (no pun intended) he needed and he pushed his cock into my mouth and held my head with both hands so that George's thrusts pushed my mouth to the base of his cock.

That's how I spent my wedding night. On a hotel bed next to the passed out bridegroom while the best man and four of the ushers took turns with me. Even though I had screwed around a lot before going to college, I'd never made it with more than one man at a time so the experience was a first for me. They all fucked me twice, a couple of them took me three times and one guy even managed to get it up four times. I lost count of how many times I had a dick in my mouth. When they left me I was one completely fucked out woman. It took me half an hour to clean up the mess - there were cum stains everywhere, even a few on Henry's arm. Henry was very apologetic when he woke up the next morning, but considering how I'd spent the night I figured the thing to do was just smile and say, "That's alright Honey. We have the rest of our lives to make love."

Naturally, I heard from "The Wedding Night Five" quite often after that night. They all wanted a repeat performance, but I was determined that I was going to be a faithful wife to Henry and in my own way I guess I was. No one ever got a cock into me during my marriage, but the 'good-time girl' in me eventually surfaced one night when I was at a party with some friends while Henry was out of town. After several drinks, a lot of close dances, and after being felt up by every man I danced with, I found myself in the back seat of Tony's car giving him and a friend of his blowjobs. Over the next couple of years, I swallowed gallons of sperm as I handed out blowjobs and hand jobs like they were party favors, mostly to 'The Five', although they were not the only ones. My boss was getting two and sometimes three a week from me (how that came about was a story in itself), but no one, except Henry, ever got a dick in me except for my mouth.

The only time I would give head (with two exceptions - one being my boss) was when Henry was out of town. The second exception was a memorable occasion. Charlie had been after me for some time to get together with 'The Five' on our fifth anniversary. At first I refused every time he brought up the subject, but, when two days before the date, Henry told me he would have to work late that night and we would have to celebrate some other time, I got pissed. I called Charlie and told him to set it up, the only conditions being that it would have to be done on my lunch hour and there would be nothing but oral sex. He agreed.

When the day arrived, I arranged for a long lunch hour and

headed for the motel. When I got there I found all five men waiting for me, naked and with hard ons ready to go. They had a cake with five candles on it, some champagne on ice, and each one gave me an anniversary card. It may sound silly, but I was touched - I thought it was very sweet of them. I excused myself and went into the bathroom where I changed and freshened up my make-up (I put on the brightest shade of red lipstick I could find). I walked back into the room wearing my wedding dress, veil, white nylons and white high heels.

What was supposed to take only an hour or so ended up taking all afternoon. The guys just kept getting hard and I was determined not to quit until they could not get it up anymore. When we finally stopped, I was covered in cum. I had swallowed a lot and a lot was splashed on me by guys standing around watching me and jacking off and then shooting all over me when they came. The boys behaved themselves for the most part and settled for blow jobs, finger fucking me, and sucking on my tits, but at one point in the festivities, while George was tit fucking me and I was giving hand jobs to Tony and Charlie, I felt my legs being moved apart and I looked to see John getting ready to fuck me. At the last minute Al pushed him away and reminded him of the agreement. I have to admit I had mixed emotions at that point. I was determined that my pussy remained Henry's only, but at that particular moment in time I was very, very ready for a hard hot cock.

Fate almost got me again. I'd just gotten home and was in the shower when Henry walked in. He had hurried to finish the job he was on and had rushed home. Five minutes earlier and I don't believe I could have explained what he would have seen.

There is one last chapter to this story. After seven wonderful years with Henry, I came home from work one day to find him dead on the kitchen floor. He'd had an embolism and it reached his brain. Following the funeral, at which Charlie and three others of 'The Five' acted as pallbearers (Tony had moved out of state) everyone came over to the house for the wake. After a night of drinking, the inevitable happened and I once again found myself as the centerpiece of a gang-bang. This time, however, I wasn't totally aware of what was happening.

It started with my 'Five' and went from there. I know that all of the pallbearers fucked me and I vaguely remember another woman sucking my tits while I was being fucked and then she was beside me getting fucked herself. I was told later that fifteen men had me that night, some of them more than once, and that both of Henry's brothers and one of his uncles were among that number.

I thus had the dubious distinction of being gangbanged in both my wedding dress and my widow's weeds.

The End
****

Here is a sample from another story you may enjoy:

Erotica Short Stories, vol.22

Explicit Stories In 1

Just Plain Bob

What I Want To Do To Her

I had a scowl on my face when I hung up the phone. I did not like Julie, never had, never would. She was just a little too wild and free for my taste. She had been married three times and even though I had never been able to confirm it (Bev flatly denied it was true) I'd heard that the reason for the divorces was that Julie had been caught playing around. I didn't know if it were true or not, but there was just something about her that set my teeth on edge. But she was Bev's best friend so there wasn't much I could do about it except live with it.

Julie stood up for Bev at our wedding and since then she and Julie had gotten together at least once a week for coffee and they were constantly on the phone with each other. It hadn't been too bad there for a while, but then things changed. The big change came when Max joined the Marines and Julie (named for Bev's friend) went off to college. With nothing much except an empty nest on her hands, Bev decided to go to work. Julie got her a job where she worked and after that they went out for dinner and drinks at least once a week and at least once a week they stopped after work for drinks with their co-workers.

While I would just as soon she not spend as much time with Julie, I did enjoy the hell out of the nights she did. She would come home and fuck my brains out. I asked her once what the deal was.

"Promise you won't get angry?"

"Don't know. When you put it like that it is like telling me that there might be something to be angry about."

"Let me back up then. You know I love you, right?"

"Yes."

"You know I wouldn't do anything to screw up what we have, right?"

"Why am I suddenly starting to feel like I'm not going to like what I'm about to hear?"

"Don't be that way, baby. It isn't bad. The reason I come home horny is because when we stop for drinks we also dance and I'm a good looking girl even if I do say so myself. I get hit on a lot and when I dance with the guys who ask me I get felt up a lot. I never let it go anywhere, but it does wind me up and as soon as I get home to you you have to unwind me."

"That's the nights you stop after work, but what about the nights when it is just you and Julie?"

"Same thing. We eat and then go to a lounge for drinks. Guys start moving in on us and we let them buy us drinks and dance with us and they wind me up and you get the benefit."

She saw the look on my face and said, "Come on, baby, I've never even so much as kissed one of them. I let them buy me drinks and I dance with them. They rub up against me, cop a feel of my boobs, run their hands over my ass and I let them because I know I'm getting them hot and I'm going to leave them hanging. They all can see my rings and they try to come on to me anyway so I feel they deserve to be left with a case of blue balls. Honest, baby, I'm just having fun and you get to reap all the benefits."

It was true, I was reaping plenty of benefits. As with a lot of married couples, as we got older we had slipped into a rut. The frequency of our lovemaking had diminished to once a week and sometimes even once every two weeks. My sex life had dramatically improved once Bev had gone back to work. So I kept my dislike of Julie to myself, the same as I had for the last twenty years.

If you enjoyed this sample then look for **<u>What I Want To Do To Her</u>**.

Also by this Author:

Becoming a Shared Husband, Vol. 1 –

(Suck Me)

Becoming a Shared Husband, Vol. 2 –

(Husbands Who Stray)

Becoming a Shared Husband, Vol. 3 –

(Get even!)

Becoming a Shared Couple, Vol. 1 –

(Steamy Swingers)

Becoming a Shared Couple, Vol. 2 –

(The Share Thing)

Becoming a Shared Couple, Vol. 3 –

(Kathy is Wild)

Erotica Short Stories, Vol. 1 –

(Taboo Desires)

Erotica Short Stories, Vol. 2 –

(Nasty Steps)

Erotica Short Stories, Vol. 3 –

(Married But…)

Erotica Short Stories, Vol. 4 –

(Sizzling 10)

Erotica Short Stories, Vol. 5 –

(In My Wife's Panties)

Erotica Short Stories, Vol. 6 –

(Taboo Unlimited Desires)

Erotica Short Stories, Vol. 7 –

(XXX Stories)

Yes, I write about sluts and whores because as everyone knows, you tend to write about the things you know. And I do like sluts and whores, just not the ones that lie to me and cheat on me.

So be forewarned - if you click on a Just Plain Bob story you will be getting sluts, whores and husbands who do not kill, maim and destroy. There are other things you will rarely find in a Just Plain Bob story.

If you enjoyed any of my books then please share the love and promote my books in Amazon. I would really appreciate your honest reviews, too!

Good news is always welcome.

One Last Thing, For Kindle Readers...

When you turn the page, Kindle will give you the opportunity to rate this book and share your thoughts on Facebook and Twitter. If you enjoyed my writings, would you please take a few seconds to let your friends know about it? Because... when they enjoy they will be grateful to you and so will I.

Thank you!

Just Plain Bob
justplainbob@awesomeauthors.org

You may also like the books by these authors:

***

"Why don't we go out tonight?" Adam suggested to his wife, Keri.

"If you want to," Keri agreed. "Any special reason or place in mind?"

"Actually, yes," Adam replied. "It's a special sort of place, private."

"What's it like?" Keri asked, intrigued.

"I don't really know, except that there are special costume requirements for women," Adam told her. "I heard about it at work from some of the guys."

"What kind of special requirements?" Keri asked.

"A special mask," Adam explained.

"Where do we get it?" Keri inquired.

"Well, actually one of the guys gave me one, just in case, you know," he replied lamely.

"So, let's see it," Keri said, crooking her head sideways as she looked at her husband.

Slowly Adam reached into his briefcase and withdrew the mask.

"Oh, my," Keri said, her eyes widening in surprise as she reached for it. "This is different," she commented as she held it up and looked at it. "What is this supposed to be?" she asked, indicating a mouthpiece-like part with a ball on the other end.

"You put that part in your mouth," Adam explained.

"How do you know this?" Keri asked, a twinkle in her eye.

"They showed me how it works," Adam told her. "I didn't know either."

"So show me," Keri told him, holding it out.

"Well, it's like this," Adam said, reaching up and pulling the mask over her head. It covered her eyes and nose with the mouthpiece filling her mouth. There was a good-sized hole through the mouthpiece making it possible to breath. Adam fastened the laces in the back and tightened the mask. Now Keri couldn't see or talk and Adam noticed that her breathing rate was increasing. Keri reached up with her hands and felt around the mask, feeling the soft leather and trying to control her panic at having been stricken blind and dumb in one fell swoop. When she reached behind her head for the laces, Adam quickly untied them and helped her out of the mask.

"Wow, that's some sensation," Keri said when Adam had removed the mask. "And I'd have to wear that?"

"That's the rules," Adam told her. "If you take it off you have to leave."

"Wow! It sounds really strange," she said. "Is this something that you want to do?" Keri asked him.

"Only if you want to," Adam told her. "It sounded pretty kinky to me when they told me about it."

"They've been, obviously," Keri commented. "How did their wives like it?"

"Well, he said they'd been back since, so I guess she did," Adam replied.

"Well, if you'll take good care of me I'll go and see what it's like," Keri said, smiling at him. "What else should I wear?"

"Well, I heard there's dancing, so something comfortable for that."

"It'll be strange dancing blind," Keri commented. "But it could also be sort of neat too, I guess. Let's go change," she said, turning towards their bedroom.

It only took them about ten minutes to dress. Keri wore what she usually wore to go out dancing, a short skirt and a halter top. Her full breasts filled the halter top and her skirt came only one third of the way down her thighs. She had nice long legs and she knew she looked good. Instead of her usual high heels, though, she was wearing a pair of sensible flat shoes.

"Dancing blind, you know," she said in way of explanation.

"You look great," Adam told her, meaning it.

He thought she was the hottest looking woman on the planet and he loved it when she dressed hot to go out. As they went to the car and began driving to the party, Adam was filled with trepidation. There was more about the party that he knew that he hadn't told Keri about. He'd had this secret desire for a long time and hadn't known how to act on it until now. He just hoped that Keri would go along and not freak out.

It only took them about 20 minutes to get to where they were going, a big beautiful house in the section of the city reserved for very rich people. Keri was suitably impressed as they turned into the drive and saw about a dozen other cars already parked there. When they parked, Adam pulled out the mask and held it out to her.

"Are you sure you want to do this?" he asked once more.

"Why not?" Keri asked, taking it from him. "What's the worst that can happen?"

To buy this book, look for <u>Naughty Swingers by George X. Bush</u>.

***

THREESOMES EROTICA
DOUG AND DIANE SERIES, BOOK 2

AND MASSEUSE
Makes Three

IAN MACSWAIN

I am a professional masseuse, and have been for many years. When I say professional, I mean that I do massage strictly with no funny business, or hanky panky. My husband is a successful businessman, so I don't have to work as hard as some of my other LMT friends, but I take my work very seriously. My kids are old enough so that my not being at home when they get home from school is not an issue anymore either. This allows me the freedom to set a pretty flexible schedule.

I have a pair of clients, a husband and wife couple, that I have been massaging for quite a number of years. Doug and Diane are a very active couple with two kids in junior high school. Doug designs websites and Diane owns a floral shop. They do very nicely. Their house is up in the hills on about 10 acres of land, with a spectacular view. We have gotten very friendly over the years, like old friends. When I go to massage them, we usually sit and talk for awhile and have a glass of wine on the deck. They are such regular clients that I leave one of my massage tables at their house; they dedicated a room to it. Our relationship has always been totally professional.

Until recently.

A couple of weeks ago, I got a call from Doug, on the morning of one of our appointments, asking if he could meet me for lunch. This was a bit of an irregular request but we had become close enough client/friends that I agreed and we met at a nice restaurant near his office. We chatted for awhile, about family stuff, some business chit chat until he got around to the point and mentioned their upcoming 17th anniversary; coming up the following weekend. They had both agreed that they wanted to do something really special. Doug seemed very nervous. I asked him what was wrong.

"This is really tough to say," he stammered. "And I don't want to make you feel weird." He paused a while before continuing. "Diane and I both really enjoy your company. We think of you as a good friend, as well as our health professional." I told him that I considered them more than simply clients. "Well, we wanted to,...well, ask you if..." He trailed off again.

"I'm not following." I told him.

"We really don't want to risk our friendship with you." He said slowly. "We wanted to know if...you would consider...getting closer."

"Closer?" I asked, unsure what he meant.

"Well, at the risk of offending you, ..." He was starting to hem and haw about our earlier discussion about professionalism with my work, keeping it totally professional. "We were wondering if you would consider indulging us in a more,... sensual,... kind of massage."

"More sensual?" I asked. "You mean sexual?"

"No, no." He stumbled. "Well, unless..." There was a long look between us, wherein I said nothing.

"This is not going, ... you know, forget it. I'm sorry if, ..." We shared a long fairly awkward silence. I think I know what he was saying, and with any other person, I would be up and out of there already. I knew these people, though. This was not something that would drive me out of my chair as I thought it might. I really liked them and Doug was really embarrassed now.

"Hey. It's okay." I told him, trying to prevent him having the heart attack he appeared to be having. I admit that I was intrigued as to what they might be considering, as a couple. It was their anniversary after all. "Just tell me what's on your mind."

"Diane was in a panic over being the one to ask, but now I wish she was here, ..." I simply waited, trying not to look as flustered as I felt. I had only had to deal with these kinds of come-ons a couple of times, and had simply packed my shit and walked out; perhaps a bit stern a response but I wasn't having this discussion with strangers, men.

"Diane and I both really like you. We both think that you're awesome at what you do. And ... honestly ... we both find you very attractive, and we have both been considering ... you know ... a ... something different." Doug's hands were fluttering as if trying to not say something too outlandish. "Not that you ...", he stammered. I smiled at him.

"When I started in this line of work, I swore that I would never get involved in anything sexual with my clients." He looked a bit sad and ashamed for asking. "Don't get me wrong, I'm very flattered that you are asking. I think that you are both very attractive. Very! I suppose if I was ever to consider something like that, it would probably be with people like you two."

"But, ..." he trailed off. "I hope that you're not offended."

"No. Truly."

"I'm sorry. I really am. I hate to make you feel uncomfortable." I assured him that it was fine; that I wasn't, though secretly I was. My mind was suddenly filled with thoughts of what they might be thinking. I caught myself flashing on both their bodies. I had been their massage therapist for a while and had seen most of them already. Diane's bottom flashed into my mind, unbidden. I had to shake my head to clear it. "Will you still make our appointment tonight?"

I patted his hand. "Of course. Believe me. It's okay." He remained uncomfortable through the rest of lunch and seemed ready as hell to get out of there. The conversation was perfunctory at best; the kids' schooling, the weather; it was agony. I tried to think of something to ease his mind. I didn't want them to be embarrassed for their appointments tonight. He shook my hand rather mechanically when we stepped out onto the street, and he walked away rather briskly. I felt so bad for him. Why I didn't feel worse for myself, I don't know.

I didn't mention my lunch to my husband when I got home, as there wasn't enough time to really get into it. The kids needed feeding and then homework had to be done. I left them in front of the TV as I headed out. Later that evening when I got to their house, I felt like Diane in particular was really embarrassed. It remained that way until we were alone and I was massaging her.

I worked on her in silence until I asked, "Are you okay?"

"Yeah, I'm fine. Why?"

"You seem so quiet."

"Oh, I'm sorry. It's just that … well, I'm a little embarrassed." I asked her about what.

"Well, having Doug ask you to help us with our little … fantasy."

"Oh, please. Don't be embarrassed. Besides, we didn't really get into that much detail."

"I'm sorry for putting you on the spot like that."

"Please don't be." I told her quietly. "Besides, I'm flattered." There was a very long silence for a while, then I asked her, "I was just caught a bit... off guard." She apologized again. I just... keep my business, well... like a business." She said that she totally understood and that she hoped I wouldn't think them weird or anything. "Oh, not at all. What people do behind closed doors..." I was sounding like I was discussing it like I knew their private life. I dropped it.

There was a very long period of silence, while I continued her shoulders and back. "I just don't want you to have the wrong idea about us." She said finally.

"I don't have any idea... It's between you guys."
"It's just a stupid fantasy kind of thing." I didn't ask what. "Perhaps they are better as fantasies anyway." She said at last. I hummed that maybe so. I finished her legs and then held the sheet for her as she rolled over.

"What is your fantasy?" I suddenly blurted, not meaning to. We remained silent for awhile. She then quietly and haltingly told me how they had discussed getting a sensual massage. She was nervous about the details, so I continued to press her gently. She described a scene with soft sexy music, dim lights and lots of candles, and a sexy scene wherein a female masseuse would be topless or nude, and there would be a lot of intimate touching, between all of them. I admitted to myself that it sounded kind of cool and that my husband Josh would probably love such a thing.

She continued that Doug would help massage Diane and then vice versa. She even admitted to being curious about being with another woman. She must have talked for half an hour about what she would like to try and watch her husband try. I told her that that sounded like a magical anniversary. She admitted that maybe they should keep it as just a fantasy. I asked her if they did want to fulfill this fantasy what they would do about making it happen. She thought they might call an escort service. We left it at that.

Throughout the rest of her massage and Doug's, I kept thinking about them and the way they looked nude. Doug was silent the entire time. I was becoming intrigued with the idea of them wanting to try something new and erotic; do it together and share the experience. Even after I left their house, I couldn't get it out of my head. When I got home, the kids were asleep and Josh was reading in bed. I mentioned it to my husband, who was already half-asleep. He told me that it sounded like fun to him, and that I might enjoy it. He rolled over and turned out the light, but that comment kept me up half the night. It sounded like fun to him. And what did he mean I might enjoy it?

If you enjoyed this sample then look for <u>And Masseuse Makes Three by Ian MacSwain</u>.

***

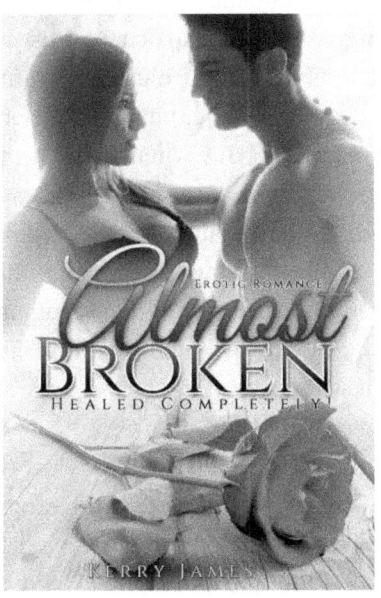

Where does life take us? Why is it that when you have settled on one course, fate comes knocking at your door and takes you off on a tangent? That's what happened to me, it seems to keep happening to me.

I get used to my life, and then fate throws a surprise my way. Sometimes it is a little tap-tap on the door, at others it's a loud knock. Sometimes it blows the door open, and when it is really serious fate just takes the thing off with its hinges.

I am Jack Hunter. My life to date had been particularly uneventful, although that would depend on your point of view. I had a wife, and a daughter. I also had an affair which while it didn't become the reason for my divorce, soured me sufficiently to seek to split with my wife. I will hold my hand up and acknowledge that I cheated on my wife. Not a good thing to do, but I will say in my defence that because my wife was in love with the bottle; Vodka and Tonic was her favourite so no one could be actually sure whether she was tippling or not; our love life was virtually zero. It's no easy task to make love to someone who reeks of alcohol. Brenda, my wife didn't appear to be bothered by our lack of intimacy, her next drink was far more important. I tried to get her to admit the problem, her Doctor tried, her mother tried, even our daughter, Libby, only three years old but she understood that something was wrong with mummy. Nothing worked. Despair and frustration were taking my self-esteem to new depths so when I had met a rather lovely lady called Deborah it quickly went from acquaintance to friendship to lovers. Our affair went on for three years. But when I called quits on my marriage, and as you would expect got taken to the cleaners in the resulting divorce, Deborah made it plain that we were not going to be an item. She came round for the sex but nothing else. Sounds like any man's dream, doesn't it? I had sex on tap and no emotional baggage to go with it. But I was one of those men who wanted emotion in a relationship, so eventually I told her it was over.

The legal process in the UK was slow but exacting. It had however problems in making its judgments effective. I had visiting rights with my daughter, which were denied or delayed for spurious reasons. My solicitor would petition the court again and again to enforce the judgment. The court would confirm the judgment but never took action to ensure it was complied with. So slowly I lost touch with my daughter.

I met Jasmine in a supermarket; I actually helped her with the heavy bags. We had coffee, then dinner and eventually we started sleeping together on occasional nights. We went on like this for five years, until one day I got a fixed penalty speeding fine in the post. The location was not one I had driven through for months, so I queried the penalty. The bloody camera was right, it was my car, but at the time I had been away at a trade show, and I had travelled to the show by train. There was only one person who had access to my house, and the keys to the company car. Jasmine! After a lot of heated arguments she admitted she had 'borrowed' the car. Problem was that she was not insured to drive it, a criminal offence in the UK. If she admitted the offence to the police, chances were that she would certainly be banned from driving, and get a hefty fine. There was also an outside chance of a prison sentence. I paid the fine, took the points on my licence, and Jasmine became history.

A few months after that lesson, I was invited to a party at a friend's house, which was where I met Bridget. We were under no illusions that we had been invited by well-meaning friends who thought that being single was an offence against nature. Well we did hit it off. Remaining friends for nearly ten years, but the tingle was just not there.

If you enjoyed this sample then look for <u>**Almost Broken by Kerry James**</u>.

***

CELIA FALKOR
A NERDY EROTICA

DELECTABLE
COLLECTABLE

Stella heard Patrick knock on the bathroom door. "Can't I get a peek?" he pleaded.

She smiled and turned the lock, "I'm not ready yet. Be patient." Stella pulled up the zippers on her black boots and fastened the small, scalloped cape. Leaning forward, she examined her hair in the mirror. It was long, straight, and strawberry blonde.

But just to be sure that her bright mane looked top-notch, she ran a comb through it one last time. Then gingerly she put her mask on, hoping that its elastic band wouldn't push any stray strands in an ungainly direction. Glancing at the mirror again, she did a spin, making her black skirt billow beneath her yellow belt. Stella grinned, "Fabulous. Patrick?"

"Yeah honey?"

"Get ready for the reveal..." Unlocking the door, she opened it a crack and stuck one leg out, bending it sensually before kicking the door wide open. "What do you think?"

Patrick leaned against the wall, and let out a low whistle. "I don't think there'll be a sexier Batgirl found in the whole convention tomorrow."

Stella stepped up to him and gave him a light peck on the lips before running a finger along his shaved head. "Even if there was, I'm sure she'd be quite jealous of the strapping young man on my arm. Did the front desk have a catalog for the auction?"

"Yes."

"Well then, let's take a look."

"First you have to find it."

"Hide and seek?" Stella cracked her knuckles. "This shouldn't be too difficult." She turned and began an inspection of the hotel room, looking back at Patrick every so often to catch him staring at her bat-clad form. The catalog wasn't in or on the nightstand; wasn't under the bed, in the sheets, or among the pillows; and wasn't behind the TV or mini-fridge. "If you're going to enjoy the show, you might as well give me a hint."

"I can tell you that you're very cold."

"Am I?" Stella took a step toward Patrick.

"Now you're getting warmer."

Stella took a few more steps before standing nose-to-nose with him. "How warm am I now?" she whispered.

Patrick buried his face in her hair. "Red hot." Stella put one hand on his brawny chest and slid the other into his pants.

"Found it!" She pulled the rolled-up UltraCon catalog from its hiding place and hopped onto the bed. As she flipped through the glossy pages, Patrick lied down beside her and put his arm over her shoulder. Stella bit her lip as her eyes scanned the auction items listed, "Let's see... Section One: Props, Section Two: Costumes and Accessories, Section Three: Artwork, Section Four: Toys and Figurines..."

Patrick excitedly pointed to the bottom of one page, "There it is! Item 138!" The couple aimed a longing gaze at the catalog's listing: "Item 138, Princess Speer-La of Evermore figurine (with detachable skirt and spear). Limited Edition, 1982." Next to this was a photograph of the plastic princess.

She was six inches tall with long, Barbie-like hair and a painted-on leotard encrusted in ersatz jewels. She wore a silver skirt on her waist and in her right hand she wielded a spear the color of gold. "Mint condition," breathed Stella. Such preservation seemed like a miracle, given the nature of the toy's rarity. Only a thousand Speer-Las from the original line of Evermore toys had been distributed to retailers, and most of those were soon recalled when the princess's hewn cleavage sparked outrage among concerned parents.

Many of the remaining toys were discarded aimlessly by their child owners or hidden under mattresses by lusty, teenage boys. In the seven years that Stella and Patrick had been running their comic book shop, the Amazing Ashcan, they had heard of just a dozen Speer-Las still existing in the hands of private collectors. But in honor of UltraCon's twentieth anniversary, Mazda Mikkenson, the star of the 1985 *Speer-La* film, had donated her own Speer-La figurine to the convention's annual charity auction. Stella climbed onto Patrick's lap and held the open catalog in front of his face. "Where do you think it would look nice in the shop?"

"Hmmm..." As Patrick thought, his gaze wandered to Stella's bust, which was emblazoned with her costume's yellow Bat-symbol. "How about in a glass case above the counter? That way when people walk in, they can see my girl's hotter than the greatest warrior of Evermore."

Stella sat the catalog on the nightstand and turned to face him," And we can put another action figure in beside her, a stud that looks half as good as you..." She pressed her mouth onto Patrick's in a warm kiss, keeping her lips sealed even as she felt Patrick's tongue approach. He slid it along her upper and lower lip and across the seam of her mouth, poking at each corner to gain entry. His hands crept underneath her top and up to her strapless bra, where he pressed his palms against her covered breasts. Stella took a deep breath in, giving Patrick the opportunity to push his tongue into her mouth.

Her tongue laid in wait, and when they met they prodded at each other with a fury. Ripping from him and forcing his arms down, Stella began to unbutton Patrick's shirt. Once the last button had been freed, Patrick shook the shirt off and tossed it onto the floor. Stella began to lift her top off, but Patrick grasped her hands. "Not all the way. Here..."

If you enjoyed this sample then look for **Delectable Collectable by Celia Falkor**.

***

I saw her as I was pulling into the Pendleton truck stop. Even though it was unseasonably warm, it was still out of the ordinary for anyone to be wearing such short cutoff jeans. As my eyes travelled up the rest of her body, it was easy to see that she was a knock out. My jaw dropped when I finally studied her face. This girl could be an identical clone of that Claudia Black who was on that hit TV show Farscape.

Even with the dark aviator sun glasses she was wearing, I could swear they looked identical.

I tried not to stare at her when I passed her going in the door to buy some coffee and use the restroom.

I could not see her eyes through the dark sunglasses, but she seemed to have a whimsical smirk on her face as I went past her. I made it a point to keep my eyes on her face but I could still feel a wiggle down between my legs as I caught a whiff of her honeysuckle scented perfume. I was disappointed to find that she had left the sales area when I came back out to get my coffee and a snack cake.

She was standing by the curb as I was pulling out of the parking area. I saw two cars stop almost instantly but she waved them away just before I reached the exit driveway. I almost bit my tongue when I pulled up in front of her to see if she would accept a ride. I figured that was why she had her thumb out. Her black leather biker style jacket was completely unzipped in front and I could see most of both her big firm breasts.

When I pressed the button to lower the passenger window, she bent forward to peer in at me.

"Where do you need to go?" I asked her. I could not keep myself from glancing at her bare chest. "My breasts need to get as far away from here as possible," she taunted me when I glanced up into her eyes. "The rest of me would like to go along as well."

To buy this book, then look for <u>The Daring Doppelgangers by Jack Ryder</u>.